"I won't forget my promise to you, Lizzy. Got that?"

Her heart melted. His promise to protect her and to see that justice was done. She believed him, too. She wasn't sure how it had happened, but something about Isaac Yoder had reached out and broken through the wall of distrust and cynicism she had built up.

The fact that she was beginning to trust the earnest man before her terrified her.

She could not afford to let any man close to her, especially not one who seemed to understand her so well. Whatever charms Isaac Yoder possessed, no matter how charismatic or upright he was, he was a man who had chosen to leave the Amish world. So even in the unlikely circumstance that Lizzy decided to one day marry, he would never be a choice she'd be able to make.

"I will be fine. You don't need to worry about me."

Deliberately, she got into the cruiser and turned her face forward. The car started advancing. She could feel his gaze on her as the distance between them increased. It took all her will, but she never glanced back.

Dana R. Lynn grew up in Illinois. She met her husband at a wedding and told her parents she'd met the man she was going to marry. Nineteen months later, they were married. Today, they live in rural northwestern Pennsylvania with enough animals to start a petting zoo. In addition to writing, she works as a teacher for the deaf and hard of hearing and works in several ministries in her church.

Books by Dana R. Lynn

Love Inspired Suspense

Amish Country Justice

Amish Witness Protection

Visit the Author Profile page at Harlequin.com.

GUARDING THE AMISH MIDWIFE

DANA R. LYNN

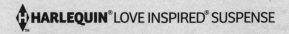

HARLEQUIN® LOVE INSPIRED® SUSPENSE

Recycling programs
for this product may
not exist in your area.

LOVE INSPIRED BOOKS

ISBN-13: 978-1-335-23215-1

Guarding the Amish Midwife

www.Harlequin.com

Printed in U.S.A.

O Lord my God, in thee do I put my trust: save me
from all them that persecute me, and deliver me.
—*Psalms* 7:1

For my husband, Brad. Thanks for supporting me
as I followed my dream.

Acknowledgments

Thanks to my children, for understanding when
Mom had a deadline and being willing to help out.

To my best friends Amy and Dee—
we need to go for coffee, soon!

To Rachel and Lee, I appreciate you all so much. And
I'm still laughing over our first Facebook Live video.

To my editor, Tina, I appreciate you so much!
Thanks for everything you do!

To my agent, Tamela,
I am so blessed to have you on my side!

To my Lord Jesus Christ,
may my work always bring You glory.

ONE

"Wait here."

Lizzy Miller watched from where she sat in the front passenger seat, stunned, as her *Englisch* hired driver, Bill Allister, shifted his car into Park in the empty lot before throwing the door open and jumping out of the vehicle, ignoring the rain that pelted him. The drops made wet smacking sounds as they hit his worn leather jacket. He left the car running as he moved toward the back door. She craned her neck to watch him, incredulous. She couldn't believe that he was planning on leaving her here, alone. But clearly, that was exactly what he had in mind as he pulled the back door open. Grabbing a bag, he slammed the door and bolted around the side of the building, never glancing in her direction.

Beyond irritated now, Lizzy waited. And waited. She glanced at the clock on the dashboard several times. Fifteen minutes went by. Then twenty. Why were they stopped here? There were no other cars around. The building in front of her was obviously abandoned. Half the roof was caved in, and the windows were broken.

Graffiti covered the exterior walls. Grass and weeds grew up through cracks in the parking lot.

Lizzy drummed her fingers on the hard plastic surface where the door met the window. Amish people did not operate motor vehicles, but instead hired *Englisch* people to drive them when their buggies were not practical. Therefore, she had made arrangements and hired a driver. Bill, however, was not the driver she had expected. She should have followed her instincts when he had shown up to take her to Ohio that morning. Lizzy had hired a woman named Sue to drive her. Sue was trustworthy, reliable and, most importantly, female. Lizzy didn't trust most men. She'd had an experience several years ago that had left her shattered and insecure, and unable to tolerate the presence of strange men.

For a while, she'd suffered panic attacks. Those had faded as time passed, but her mistrust of men had not.

So when Sue had come down with food poisoning and had sent her brother, Bill, in her place that morning, Lizzy had almost canceled her plans. Not that Bill looked like a bad person. Quite the opposite. She remembered her impression when she had first seen him a few hours earlier. Nothing about him screamed untrustworthy. He was in his twenties, maybe twenty-five or -six, she would guess. Not a man one would take a second look at on the street. His hair was a little long; it just brushed his collar. It was that undefinable shade somewhere between black and brown, but not really either. He was wearing tinted glasses, so it was hard to guess at the true color of his eyes. Just an ordinary young man doing a favor for his sick sister.

She still didn't trust him.

There were two things that convinced her to get into the car with him. First, he had a letter of apology from Sue, and she knew Sue would feel horrible if Lizzy had decided not to go due to her illness. And second, she had promised her cousin Addie that she would come and stay with her for the last month of her pregnancy and assist with the delivery. Promises had to be kept.

Lizzy glanced at the clock on the dashboard again. Bill had been gone for thirty minutes. What was left of her patience vanished. She had hired a driver to take her to Ohio, not so that she could sit in a parking lot while rain hit the windshield of the car. She gritted her teeth. She had known when she had first seen him that she would not be happy with him as her driver. Sue had always been punctual, and she had always gotten Lizzy where she needed to go on time.

She recalled when Bill had moved off the normal route. She had considered holding her silence.

Let it go, she told herself.

But she couldn't. Lizzy liked to know where she was going. Being taken somewhere against her will once was enough for her. Since that time, she always knew where she was going. In the back of her mind, she knew that it was so if she ever needed to find help, she would have landmarks and locations to rely on. Right now, she didn't have either, having never traveled to Ohio by this current route. It was more than she was comfortable with.

"Excuse me, Bill," she had shouted to be heard above the radio. She had to shout twice before he responded.

Scowling, he had reached out and pushed a button as if she were inconveniencing him, and not the other way around. The song cut off mid-word. She was grateful for the quiet. "Yeah?"

She swallowed. "Um, I was just wondering why we weren't taking I-80? That's the way Sue normally takes."

"I need to make a quick stop on the way there. An errand I need to take care of. It won't take long." He had then jabbed the button with his index finger and the raucous music again filled the car.

She had been irritated, both with him and with herself. She was especially annoyed with the lack of control she had over the entire situation. Her mood hadn't improved when the rain had started to fall in fat, heavy drops on the windshield. She'd actually cringed when the man beside her had bitten off a word that was, at best, rude.

Biting her lip, Lizzy had done her best to ignore her growing anxiety. She saw the sign welcoming them into Ohio with a sigh of relief. At least she knew they were traveling in the correct direction. When Bill pulled off into an empty parking lot, she was confused. What could he be doing here? Lizzy glanced at the clock again. Thirty-five minutes had passed since Bill had left her in this car in the middle of nowhere.

Enough was enough. Lizzy was suddenly tired of allowing her anxiety to control her actions, and her life. She firmed her jaw and reached for the door handle, deliberately ignoring the way her stomach muscles tightened and clenched at the idea of an impending confrontation. She would not back down. Whatever his errand was, Bill needed to finish it quickly or come back to it after he dropped her off at her cousin's house.

Lizzy straightened the black bonnet that covered the white prayer *kapp* she wore on her head. The bonnet would at least provide some protection from the rain. She stepped out and began to walk in the direction she'd seen Bill go. Within a minute, her cloak was soaked through. Ack! Her feet kicked up more rain onto her black stockings and the hem of her dark blue dress as she trod through the puddles. The sudden discomfort she was experiencing was just one more irritation.

Up ahead, she heard voices. Loud and angry voices. She paused; the manners her parents had instilled in her said it was rude to interrupt a conversation. Then she decided she didn't care. As she drew closer, she could hear Bill's voice raised. He sounded upset. She slowed again. Maybe she should go back and wait in the car again. No. She was done with waiting. It was bad enough that she had to travel with a man, even the brother of a friend. She just wanted to be on her way and get to Addie's house.

Determined, Lizzy walked faster.

Rounding the building, she saw Bill standing with another man. At a glance, she noted that the second man had dark hair curling around his ears. He would have been handsome, but something about him was sinister. Even as she opened her mouth to call out to Bill, the other man pulled out a gun and shot him. Shocked, she watched, frozen, as Bill crumpled to the ground. For a few seconds, her mind refused to believe what her eyes had just seen.

I cannot stay here!

Spinning on her heel, Lizzy raced back to the car, the puddles making her steps slower than they would normally have been.

The sound her feet made slapping the water was also very loud in the silence following the shooting.

Within seconds, she heard a shout from where she'd just fled. She had been noticed. She didn't slow down. The sound of running steps behind her encouraged her to run faster. She hopped into the idling car and muttered a prayer of thanksgiving. She hadn't driven since her own *rumspringa* and wasn't sure she'd be able to advance the vehicle quickly enough to escape. She hit the door locks. They clicked. The man slammed against the passenger window. Screaming, she jumped. Fury twisted his features as the man who had shot her driver pounded on the window.

He backed up. The gun was still in his hand. She knew he was going to try to shoot her, too. The adrenaline hit hard, and her heart rate sped up. She felt like she couldn't get enough air as the panic began to ratchet up in her belly. She couldn't afford to have a panic attack now.

She was not going to wait for it to happen. Thankfully, her sister, Rebecca, had taught her how to drive. Sort of. The tires squealed as she yanked the gearshift back. The car jerked forward. The front wheel rammed into the curb and the car rocked, hitting the ground again with a hard bounce.

A gunshot rang out and the back passenger window shattered.

Spinning the wheel, Lizzy pressed her foot down on the gas pedal so hard that she could feel the tires grinding into the gravel and spitting it out before the car jolted forward and sped down the road, away from the man who wanted her dead. A screech and a horn blaring behind her told her that she had cut someone off.

She kept going. The man who had shot Bill would recognize his car. She had to put as much distance between herself and the killer as possible.

Police officer Isaac Yoder sat up in his parked patrol car as a dark blue sedan that had seen better days raced toward him through the heavy rain, swerving on the wet roads. The driver went over the edge of the road and onto the shoulder three times, the way a frightened rabbit veers back and forth when trying to escape an oncoming car. At one point, Isaac was sure that he saw the vehicle's left wheels lift off the surface of the road.

The driver had to be drunk or having some sort of issue, possibly health related, like a heart attack. It was also possible that it was a teenager texting. Whatever the reason for the erratic driving, he needed to pull the car over now. No one drove that way in fair weather if they were fully competent. Add in the rain pouring down, that driver was asking to hydroplane on the slick surface. Even as he watched, the back tires hit a pool of deeper water and the back end of the car fishtailed before straightening up again.

Flipping on the siren and his lights, he pulled out from beside the overpass where he had been partially hidden as he watched the traffic. Blue-and-red flashes reflected in the puddles on the road. His hands gripped the wheel as he gave chase. It was fortunate that it was midmorning and the traffic was light. Otherwise, he had no doubt that an accident would have already occurred.

The automated plate recognition system in his cruiser alerted him that the car ahead was owned by someone with a driving record. The car he was chasing down belonged to William Allister, a young man who had multiple tickets and two DUIs already on his record. Well, he was about to get another one.

Isaac wasn't shocked when the car suddenly veered onto the narrow shoulder, although in his mind he had prepared for the scenario that Mr. Allister would try to make a run for it. A chase would not have been smart, but sometimes drivers panicked when faced with another DUI and the loss of their driver's license.

He pulled up behind the vehicle, making sure his cruiser was partially on the road. That would make drivers move to the next lane, and it would give him a safe cushion to walk to the car without being too close to it. Isaac turned off the siren, but he left the lights on. He called in the situation to his station, along with the license plate number and the driver's record. Patting his service weapon in his holster, he slowly exited his vehicle. It was always best to proceed with caution in these incidents. The last thing he wanted was for the person in the car to decide to pull a weapon on him or to attack. Given the way the guy had been driving, it would not shock Isaac if that was exactly what happened.

The rain poured down at a slant, hitting him clear in the face. He couldn't afford to duck his head as he approached the car. He blinked his eyes to clear them. He needed to be able to see, to watch for potential threats. A lone car sped past him, not even bothering to move to the other side of the road. He narrowed his eyes as the vehicle continued down the road and disappeared. No doubt the driver was going above the speed limit.

As he approached, he could see that there was only one person in the car. He didn't let himself relax. Far too often, people ducked down to hide in the floorboards. He could view into the backseat. No one was there. He scanned the rest of the vehicle. One of the back windows had been shattered. His suspicions heightened. He took a cautious step closer, enough that he could just barely make out the top of a head around the headrest. Two hands on the wheel. That was good. If he could see the hands, they weren't reaching for a weapon. He arrived at the car window and stared. Realizing his jaw had dropped open, he closed it with a click.

William Allister might have owned the car, but he certainly wasn't driving it. Inside the car was a young Amish woman, face wet with tears. She turned her terrified, brilliant blue eyes to him. He motioned for her to roll down the window. He had to repeat the motion twice before she complied. Suspicion darted across her face, but the terror was stronger. A tiny bit of relief mingled in her expression, as well.

Isaac understood the suspicion all too well. The Amish did not, as a rule, involve the police in their business. His own *dat* had refused to go to the police at a very critical time in Isaac's life. Joshua had died, the victim of three drunk teens who had found a blind Amish youth an easy mark, and his father would not be moved to see that justice was done. Isaac pushed his memories of his younger brother from his mind. The bitterness was still too strong, even after seven years.

So was the guilt. Isaac had argued with his father, the first time in his life he had refused to give in to his *dat*'s commands. He'd been so angry, in fact, that Isaac had left his Amish community, and the Plain tradition in which he was raised, instead of being baptized in the faith. His father had died two years ago, and they had never reconciled. A circumstance that weighed heavy on his conscience every single day of his life. With his father's death, any hope he might have had of ever rejoining the Amish community that his mother and sister still lived in had also died. It didn't matter that he had not been baptized, therefore meaning he could technically maintain his ties with his community, since his father had made it very clear that if he left, he would not be welcome there anymore. He couldn't have stayed, though. He needed to find some justice for his brother. Nothing mattered until he'd accomplished that.

He pulled his mind back to the car in front of him.

The young woman finally managed to roll the window down. It was an older vehicle, so the windows were manually controlled. Judging by the way she had to resort to using both hands, they weren't in the best of condition, either. Her hands were shaking hard and her face was as pale as milk. Was she injured? He slid his glance over her, doing a rapid assessment. No visible injuries. Still, he couldn't rule out injury or illness.

She was breathing fast and shallow, he noted.

"Miss, do you need help? You're very pale, and you were driving all over the road."

When she didn't respond immediately, he asked again if she needed help, this time in the American-flavored German used by the Amish, sometimes known as Pennsylvania Dutch. He didn't even stop to think about it. It had been a while since he'd spoken that dialect.

Seven years, to be exact.

Her dark blue eyes widened. She finally responded, though. "*Jah*, I need help."

She burst into sobs again, burying her face in her hands. Her shoulders heaved. All he could see now was the black bonnet on her head. He frowned. Her cloak looked wet. She must have been out in the rain. Leaning over slightly, he saw the seat on the other side of her was drenched. Yep, she had definitely been out in the downpour.

An unlikely thought occurred to him. He was pretty sure she wouldn't have stolen a vehicle, but there was still a slight possibility that she had.

"Um, ma'am, this car, did you, um, borrow it?" He didn't want to outright ask her if she took it.

She lifted her face and bobbed her head. "*Jah*, I did borrow it. My driver, Bill, got out to do something, and he left me in the car for a long time. I got tired of waiting for him, so I went to find him. He was with another man. They were arguing. The other man shot him. I think he's dead."

TWO

Isaac's eyes scanned the oncoming traffic for any visible threats. He didn't see any, but that didn't mean anything. Right now, he was an open target for anyone who was after the young woman in front of him. Isaac didn't question whether or not she was making up the story. He doubted she could fake terror that deep. Even if she were making up the story, though, he still had a duty to check it out.

"You can't sit out here in the open. And I need to get the details. Can you come back to my car? I want to call in some backup, too."

She hesitated. For a moment, he was sure she would refuse. She surprised him when she nodded and stepped from the car. Isaac moved to her side and cupped her elbow in his palm as they walked back to his police cruiser. He wanted to make sure she didn't slip and fall, but he also wanted to hurry her along so that she was in plain view for as short a time as possible. As long as she was out in the open, she was vulnerable. He kept her along the shoulder, keeping himself between her and anyone passing by.

If someone was going to play target practice with them, hopefully they would hit him first and give her time to flee. Isaac didn't even think of not protecting her. It was just the way things had to be. The area between his shoulder blades itched. He could almost imagine the crosshairs of a scope lining up.

He increased his pace. She kept up with him. For a little thing, she was quick. Her head barely came to his shoulders, and he was only five foot ten.

A minute later, Isaac squired her into his vehicle.

The young woman shifted in her seat. It wasn't difficult to tell that being in a police car was not something she was comfortable with. He wished he could make it easier for her, but it was just something she would have to deal with. Isaac was not unsympathetic. He remembered very well the first time he had dealt with the police. Uncomfortable was a mild way of putting it.

Another quick glance out the window assured him that no one with a gun was bearing down on them. He blew out a breath, relieved. He had never been shot in the line of duty, not in the two years he had been a police officer. He would prefer to keep it that way.

Turning his attention back to his passenger, he squelched the pity that he instinctively felt as he viewed the red-rimmed blue eyes. His whole focus needed to be on keeping her safe and catching the perp. That called for objectivity.

"Before you begin to tell me what happened," he said to her, "let me call in to my station. If there is some guy out there with a gun, I want more than just myself out looking for him."

She frowned, as if he had offended her a bit by what he had said. What had he said? Oh, maybe it had sounded like he didn't quite believe her. He didn't mean it that way.

Isaac quickly radioed in to the station.

"I have a possible shooting," he told the dispatcher. "Requesting backup."

"Affirmative, Isaac. What's the location of the shooting?"

He turned to the young woman sitting beside him. "Can you tell me where you were when this happened?"

She nodded her head. "I am not from here. But I do remember it was about five minutes back. There was an old abandoned place. It was a large blue building. The windows were all broken out." She bit her lip. "I am sorry. That is all I can remember."

Isaac flashed her a brief smile. "It's fine. Believe it or not, that helps a lot." He pushed the button for the radio again. "Maureen, I have reason to believe that the shooting was at the Carstairs place."

"Gotcha, Isaac," Maureen said on the other end of the line. "I have Ryder heading out your way. He should be there in under ten. You hold on."

"Will do. Could you also send out a tow truck? We need the car towed into evidence." He waited for her to answer in the affirmative and then he disconnected the call. The young woman beside him was staring out the window, her eyes scanning the road. "All right. Another officer will be here soon. I am Officer Isaac Yoder with the Waylan Grove Police Department. Why don't you start from the beginning? Who are you and what you were doing when all of this happened?"

She gave the surrounding area one more sweep before focusing her large blue eyes on his face. Her black bonnet was sagging on her head. Only a hint of pale blond hair peeped out from under it. She cleared her throat. Her voice, when she spoke, was soft. He was surprised that she kept it steady. It was obvious to him that her anxiety had not lessened.

"My name is Elizabeth Miller. Lizzy. I live outside LaMar Pond, a small town in northwestern Pennsylvania. I am training to be a midwife."

She flushed. A smile nearly slipped out of him. He remembered that women did not talk about things such as having babies and pregnancy in front of strangers, and especially not in front of men. He'd been living in the *Englisch* world so long he'd almost forgotten that.

"I know where LaMar Pond is. Go on."

"My cousin Addie asked me to visit her here in Ohio." She paused, as if trying to decide how much to tell him. "My normal driver was sick, so her brother, Bill, showed up to drive me."

Bill. William Allister. He sat up straighter in his seat.

"Had you met Bill before?"

She shook her head, her nose wrinkling. "I do not hire men to drive me around. I would not have gone with him, but I knew that I needed to get to my cousin's house. I had promised her, and it was too late to change plans. Besides, I didn't want my regular driver, Sue, to feel bad."

Distress shadowed her face. It didn't take much

imagination to know that she was thinking about how the poor woman would feel when she found out what had happened to her brother. He blocked an image of his own brother's face from surfacing. That was twice in one day he'd thought of Joshua's death.

"I am sorry about the delay, Lizzy. I will try to get you to your cousin's house as soon as I can. I promise."

She shrugged it off. "I got in the car. We drove for a while. I noticed that Bill was going a back route. One that I wasn't as familiar with. I was annoyed with him."

She seemed ashamed of that now.

"He said he had an errand to run. When he stopped, he told me to wait in the car. And I did. I waited for a long time. Over thirty minutes. When he didn't come back, I got impatient and went to find what was taking him so long."

In the quiet car, Isaac heard her swallow in a loud gulp.

"I went behind the building. I could hear voices arguing, but I was so irritated that I did not pay attention to what they were saying. I saw Bill. He was facing another man. The other man had a gun. He shot him. He shot him!"

Her voice rang with horror. Isaac could only imagine how shocking that must have been, for her to witness such an awful thing.

"You saw him shoot Bill?" He wanted to be certain he had the facts correct.

She nodded. "I saw Bill fall. I was so scared I ran back to the car. Bill had left it running. The man shot out the back window."

She pointed to the rear passenger seat with an unsteady finger. He recalled the shattered window. He would need to get this car into the station so that it could be searched for the bullet. Or other evidence. It would not be safe to try to process the car on the side of the road with a possible killer searching for her.

"Then what happened? After he shot out the window."

"I drove away as fast as I could. I have only driven a couple of times, for fun. I haven't driven at all since I was baptized two years ago. I know that the man will come after me. He was running to his car when I reached the street."

He was sure that he would come after her, too. Right now, he had a possible dead body, a single witness and the murdered man's car. Oh, yeah. There was a very good chance that someone would come after this young woman to shut her up.

It was his job to make sure they failed.

He spoke quietly, calmly. "I know it was horrible, Lizzy. But I need a description of the man who shot Bill."

Lizzy squeezed her eyes shut, as if she could force herself to forget the events of the day. He knew the feeling. "He had dark curly hair. Dark brown eyes. I'm certain that I would know him if I saw him again."

He frowned as he considered what he knew. "The man, do you think he got a good look at your face? Could he recognize you?"

He had to assume that he had, but he knew that to many *Englischers*, all they would notice was the *kapp* and the dress. With her black bonnet on, it was possible that the man wouldn't have gotten a good look at her.

Her nod was emphatic, tearing that hope to shreds. "For a moment, before he shot out the window, he looked directly into my eyes. He chased me, too, in his car. When you pulled me over, he continued past us."

The only car to pass them had been the one that he'd thought he'd been sure had been speeding. Unfortunately, he had not been able to get a plate number or even much information in regard to the make and model of the vehicle. Determined to pay attention and get all the details he could from the witness, he turned back to her. Her wide blue eyes were pinned to his face. She let out a sound that was half sigh, half strangled sob.

"I think if you had not pulled me over, he would have caught up with me and killed me, too."

Within minutes, Lizzy saw lights flashing in the side mirrors of Isaac's police car. The backup he had called for had arrived. She was glad, but she also squirmed internally, uncomfortable at once again having to deal with the *Englisch* police. The other officer drew over to the shoulder, pulling behind Isaac's car. The lights remained on, splashing blue and red in a steady pattern against the interior of the car.

"I'll be right back." Isaac got out of the car and sauntered over to the other officer. She twisted her neck around and watched the two men talking. Both of them scanned the road. A time or two, they glanced in her direction.

This is the second time today I have been left waiting

in a car. She shook her head at the ridiculous thought. This time, Lizzy did not mind being in the car alone. It gave her the opportunity to gather her thoughts and compose herself.

Lord, help me be calm. Still my heart.

Lizzy was drained by the morning's events. Would she ever be able to forget the sight of Bill's body falling, crumpling to the ground in a heap? Or the cold face of the man who shot him? She shuddered as his face filled her mind. Poor Sue. Her friend would be devastated. Although Lizzy had not had the best impression of Bill in the few hours she'd known him, she knew that Sue had adored her younger brother. She had talked about him every time they'd traveled together.

And now he was gone.

Hugging her arms around herself, she shivered, a mixture of cold and the reaction to the morning's events setting in. Her eyes sought out Isaac, the one thing that had steadied her through the dreadful past hour.

Then she rebuked herself. She was being silly. *Gott* had brought her through it. Isaac had just been the means that *Gott* had used.

Isaac had been Plain once. He didn't have to tell her that. With a name like Yoder, there was a possibility, of course. But when he had spoken to her in the language of the Plain folk, she had been astonished. What had driven him from his community to become something so foreign to their culture as a police officer? She would never ask, of course. Such things were personal, and frequently painful.

Not that she had anything against the police. Her sister, Rebecca, was married to a very fine young police officer, Sergeant Miles Olsen. In fact, Miles had saved Rebecca and Lizzy's life several years ago. Four years ago, to be exact, when Lizzy had been almost seventeen. A man who had held a grudge against her older sister and some of Rebecca's friends had started attacking them one by one. He had killed one of them. Then he had kidnapped Rebecca and Lizzy together. She would never forget being held hostage in that cold, damp basement by the brutal man, not knowing if they would survive. Miles Olsen was an officer with the LaMar Pond Police Department. He had been on the case and had been assigned to work with Rebecca. It had made sense. Rebecca was profoundly deaf, and Miles was raised by his deaf grandparents and uncle, which meant he was fluent in American Sign Language, or ASL, and could communicate with Rebecca, while the other officers needed an interpreter to talk with her.

When she and Lizzy had been taken, Miles had rescued them. He had also been promoted to sergeant for his outstanding work and heroic efforts. He and Rebecca were now married and had a small son. Miles was perfect for Rebecca. *Gott* had provided her with a man who could protect her and communicate with her. Lizzy was very happy for her sister. She had met several of his police officer friends, too. They were all a nice group of men and women.

But that did not mean she was comfortable asking the police for assistance. She did not have a choice, though. A man had killed Bill, her driver's brother. The Amish might not turn to the police for help normally, but the *Englischers* did.

For Sue, she had to do what she could to cooperate and help them find the killer.

Another thought crossed her mind. What if this man that shot Bill found her? Memories of being chained up in a basement with her sister and another woman flooded her mind, causing a visceral reaction. Cringing away from the memories, she realized that she was pushing herself back against the seat of the car.

She could not allow herself to dwell on those memories. It would only unsettle her. Pressing a hand against her stomach, Lizzy tried to will away the queasiness and the sick feeling that arose whenever she remembered those past events. The man who had kidnapped her was in jail. He was never going to get out. She knew that. He had been charged with several counts of murder and assault. She needed to stop letting these memories and fears have so much control over her.

Lizzy did the only thing she could do and pushed the thoughts out of her mind, distracting herself with watching Isaac and his friend. It helped. For now. As she watched, a tow truck pulled in front of Bill's car and the driver hopped out. He began to hook up the car. Soon he had the car secured and was off. The moment seemed surreal. Just a few hours before, she'd been a reluctant passenger in the car because the driver was a man, and now he'd been shot before her eyes.

Within ten minutes, Isaac returned. He buckled his seat belt and tossed her an absentminded smile. Again, the question rose to mind: Why had he become a cop?

It wasn't hard to imagine him wearing a straw hat and dressed Plain. Even with the gun at his side and the fancy uniform, there was something about him that radiated Plain.

Isaac pulled away from the curb. "We are going to go a mile down the road and turn around. Then we will head back to the Carstairs place. Check out the scene. I am hoping that you will be able to identify the body, and maybe even give us a better description of the shooter. I hope you will be willing to identify him."

She could hear the question he was not asking. Would she be willing to come in and work with the police?

"*Jah*, I hope so, too."

His shoulders relaxed. He had expected her to refuse. "I am happy to hear that you will help us out."

She hesitated. How much should she tell him? "I am going to help you because of Bill's sister. Sue is a kind woman, and she dotes on her brother. It will devastate her when she learns what has happened."

He pursed his lips. Lizzy sensed that he wanted to ask more questions. For whatever reason, he did not ask. Maybe he didn't want to scare her off. Or maybe he wanted to see what they found before he got more information from her. Whatever his reasoning, she was glad that he restrained himself. She didn't have any more information, and right now, she was feeling close to screaming.

When he reached out to turn the heat up, his hand accidentally brushed against hers. She jumped and jerked her hand away. Heat crawled up her cheeks as he frowned, his brows furrowed. No doubt he was wondering at her extreme reaction.

This was why she would never get married. Even the most innocent interactions with men set her on edge. To have a normal conversation with a man who came to court her...*nee*, it would not happen. Lizzy had long ago resigned herself to the fact that what Chad Weller had done to her had left her with too many emotional scars to ever consider courting and later marrying any man. She just did not have the ability to get past her fears.

It was likely she never would.

The car turned. Lizzy became aware that they were entering the parking lot that she had fled less than two hours earlier. The building came into view as they drove into the lot. The broken windows. The whole forlorn look of the place. When she had first seen the building, she had thought it looked pitiful and broken. Now, seeing it through the eyes of the horrible situation, she thought she could detect a menacing feel to the structure and the empty lot.

She shuddered.

"Are you all right?" Isaac's concerned voice broke through the thoughts. She had almost forgotten that she wasn't alone.

"*Jah.* I am well," she whispered, even though she felt far from well. A man had died before her eyes. How was she supposed to feel?

The other officer pulled in and parked next to Isaac.

Lizzy got out when the men did. Her plain boots made a crunching sound. She flicked a glance down. She was stepping on glass.

"I think this is the glass from Bill's car window. It shattered when the other man shot at me as I was leaving."

Immediately, Isaac took a picture of the glass with his phone, then carefully picked up a shard and put it in a plastic bag with a zip seal top.

"Hopefully, we can match this to the car you were in. Although glass is pretty similar."

She shrugged, not familiar with any of the technology.

Dread started to build inside her as they moved toward the back of the building. She didn't want to see Bill's body. The thought of how he would look dead was enough to make her ill.

She turned the corner and blinked.

"Where did Bill fall?" Isaac asked, glancing around with a frown.

She pointed her finger at the spot ahead of her.

The body was gone.

THREE

Isaac walked forward to where the body should have been. It was hard to tell if a body had been there. The black pavement was slick, and the rain had probably washed most of the traces of blood away. His gut instinct told him that there had been a body here, that Lizzy really had witnessed someone getting shot.

"Maybe Bill wasn't killed?" There was a lilt in Lizzy's voice that spoke of hope. "Maybe he is hiding from the man who shot him."

He hated to dampen her hope, but he refused to downplay the danger she could be in. "Lizzy, I doubt he survived. How close were they standing when Bill was shot?"

The hope drained from her face. She sighed, a sound that seemed to be dragged up from the depth of her soul. "They were only a couple of feet apart. Maybe from me to where the other officer is standing."

About three feet, then.

"This other officer is Officer Ryder Howard." Isaac

indicated his friend and colleague. "At that close range, I don't think he would miss."

"Bill is dead." The lilt was gone and her voice was a flat statement.

"Most likely."

"Are you sure that this is the place?" Ryder asked, his face skeptical.

Lizzy flushed. Isaac would have thought she was embarrassed except he had seen the way her eyes had flashed. She did not like being questioned like that. No wonder. Ryder hadn't meant anything by it, but his voice did have a sarcastic edge to it. Lizzy had no way of knowing, but Ryder's voice always sounded that way. He doubted if the man even realized how harsh his tone was. It was just the way he talked.

"Jah!" Lizzy replied, lifting her chin, her own voice cold. "This is the place. I did not make up a story about my driver getting shot."

Ryder's eyes widened. Too late the man seemed to realize that his question had been taken the wrong way. "Oh! Hey! I didn't mean that to sound like I thought you were lying. I just wanted to make sure there wasn't a mistake."

He threw Isaac a "Help me, buddy" glance.

"It's okay, Lizzy. We'll keep looking. Maybe we will find some other signs of what happened here."

Ryder grunted, his head bobbing once. Isaac held back a smirk. His friend had gotten himself into trouble on more than one occasion for attitude. The man had a good heart. He just had a bit of a chip on his shoulder. Isaac knew that he had had a very rough time growing up with alcoholic parents. Although he had never asked, wanting to respect his friend's privacy, he had always figured there was some sort of abuse or neglect that went along with it. Ryder had developed a veneer to keep people at bay.

Isaac could not fault the man for it. Not when he had his own past to overcome.

"Lizzy, we are going to have a look around to see if we can find any evidence of what happened. I need you to either stay there or wait in the car." He zeroed his gaze in on her oval face. "I mean it. If you walk around, you might trample on something. Ryder and I have done this enough to know what we are doing."

"I will wait right here." She pointed down at her feet.

He smiled. Something about her earnestness touched him, despite the terrifying situation she was in.

"Okay, then." Turning to his friend, he gestured to the right. "Why don't you search from here toward the property line, and I will go toward the building."

"Sounds like a plan." All amusement faded as he and Ryder both focused on the job before them.

The men set off in their separate directions, alert for any clue that a murder took place in the parking lot. Every once in a while, Isaac cast a concerned glance at Lizzy. Her arms were tight across her middle, and he could clearly see that she was shivering. April in Ohio was capricious. On this particular day, the temperature hadn't risen much higher than sixty and the rain was cold. He was wet clear through after a quarter of an hour. She'd been out in the weather several times that morning. And though he knew that one did not catch a cold from being wet, it was still a miserable feeling.

At one point, he had gone over to her to suggest that she wait in the car. "I can turn the heat up. There's a blanket in the trunk. It would not be much, but it might warm you up a bit."

Lizzy had looked at him for a moment. Her lips had curled at the corners in a small smile. Her eyes, though, those deep blue eyes, had remained haunted. "*Denke*, Isaac. I appreciate it. But I would not feel as safe so far away. I might be cold here, but I have two police officers close by. No one would try to harm me here."

How did one argue with that? Isaac jogged back to continue searching. In his mind, though, her words played over and over again. If he had any doubts about her telling the truth, which he hadn't, they fled. No one would stand out in the cold to feel safer if it weren't the truth, he reasoned. Plus, her eyes held far too much knowledge of the dark side of the world.

Ten minutes later, he found his first proof of the shooter's presence. A bullet had lodged in the side of the building. He ran back to his car and grabbed some tools from his trunk. Carefully, he dug the bullet out and put it in an evidence bag.

Encouraged by what he found, he continued his search, meticulously scouring every inch for any sign of disturbance.

"Yo! Isaac! Got something!" Ryder shouted across the parking lot.

Isaac hurried over, careful not to step on anything useful.

"What do you have, Ryder?"

Ryder indicated the gravel at his feet. "Something was definitely pulled through here. Something big."

Like a body. Isaac narrowed his glance at the ground. Ryder was correct. Something had been dragged through. He looked closer.

"Ryder, look here." He pointed at a spot on the ground. "I think we have blood."

Grabbing evidence bags and their phones, they went to work taking pictures and collecting samples of both the gravel and the blood. They might not be able to use them. They didn't have the fastest DNA lab available to them. Nor was DNA always reliable.

It might not have been much. Unfortunately, it was all the evidence they had.

As they were walking back toward the cars, Isaac noticed something that had escaped their notice earlier. Under the bushes, lying on the ground, was a black baseball cap.

Lizzy gasped. "That looks like the hat that Bill was wearing when he picked me up this morning."

They carefully extracted the hat from the bushes and added it to their evidence. There was an unusual design on the front. It was only partially there, though. It looked like someone had tried to rip it off, but missed some of it. Unfortunately, the part that remained was not part of any logo that he recognized.

"I can't even tell what logo this is supposed to be. Can you tell?" Isaac frowned as he pointed it out.

The other cop shook his head. "No. Not with so much of it gone. Maybe it's the logo for the place where he works. Or maybe a sports team of some kind. It's possible someone will recognize it, although I'm not sure if there's enough for that." He snapped a picture of it.

"We'll have to ask around, see if we can find anyone who recognizes it. Right now, I am going to take Lizzy into the station to see if she can identify our shooter. As long as I'm heading in that direction, I'll take this stuff back to the station."

Ryder gave him a thumbs-up. "I will start seeing if anyone recognizes this logo."

In the car, Isaac turned the heat on and handed Lizzy a blanket. "I apologize that this is taking so long. As soon as I can, I will get you to your family's house."

"I understand. If I had thought about it, I would have asked to grab my bag from the trunk before the car was towed away." She was silent for a moment. "Do you think that maybe this guy will forget about me?"

He did not want to answer that question, mainly because he didn't like the answer that he knew he had to give. However, Isaac would never lie. He despised dishonesty.

"I don't think he will forget about you, Lizzy." She turned her pale face to him. "Right now, you are the one person who can identify him. He won't forget that."

Nor was he likely to let her go.

Lizzy regretted asking the question the minute the words left her mouth. It was too late to call them back. One look at Isaac's face, though, and she knew what the answer would be. Had known it before she'd asked.

Once again, she was a target. For no other reason

than that she had been in the wrong place. She was trapped in a weird nightmare and had no choice but to let it play out before she could be free from it.

The trip to the Waylan Grove station was silent. At some point, she dozed lightly, lulled to sleep by the rhythm of the car. A hand on her shoulder startled her awake.

She sat up with a shriek, her fist flying out to defend herself.

Belatedly, she realized where she was. When she saw Isaac rubbing the side of his head, she felt guilty.

"Sorry." She had never been so mortified.

"Don't worry about it." He dropped his hand and smiled. "I should have known better than to jostle you awake like that."

"That's no excuse. I tend to startle easy."

He nodded. "I will keep that in mind."

Isaac left his side of the car, loping around to open her door. "Let's get this done."

The Waylan Grove Police Department was bigger than the LaMar Pond one, but not by much. The open desk area where the officers sat was similar, as well. They entered, and the conversation softened to a low buzz. Isaac led her past the desks and into a room near the back. He left briefly to talk with one of the other officers, then he returned. He flipped on a switch and indicated that she could hang up her cloak on the rack in the corner.

"I doubt it will dry by the time you leave, but maybe it will a little."

It was sweet of him to be so concerned about her.

A few minutes later, a female cop walked in. Lizzy looked at the bag she was carrying.

"My bag!"

The woman laughed. "Isaac said you had left it in the trunk. The chief okayed us to get it out and bring it to you. There's a bathroom across the hall. Go ahead and change into something dry."

Not waiting to hear more, Lizzy rushed over and grabbed her bag. "*Denke.* It will be good to be warm again."

Isaac and the woman laughed softly. Hurrying to the bathroom, she searched through the bag, quickly locating the items she needed. She even found a clean *kapp* to put on her head. Never again would she take dry clothes, or being warm, for granted.

When she returned to the room, Isaac pulled out a chair for her. She sat, then looked up at him expectantly.

He sighed. "Okay. I want to know if you would be willing to look through the images we have to see if you can identify the man you saw. If you can, we'll try to arrest him. Soon as that's done, you could be on your way home to your family in no time."

"I hope so. I will look at your pictures."

What she hadn't counted on was the sheer volume of pictures. It took her nearly two hours to go through each and every picture. And still, she did not find an image that matched.

"Are you sure you would recognize him if you saw him?" Isaac stood to pace the room.

"I would recognize him. I will probably have nightmares of his face for years to come. His picture is not here."

Moving back to the table, Isaac turned and leaned against it. "I believe you. I had hoped his picture would be in the database."

"*Jah*, me, too. Did I look at all the pictures?"

"Yup. That was all of them."

"What do we do? I didn't see him." She crossed her arms and rubbed her hands up and down them, shivering slightly, although not from being cold.

"The visual artist will be in tomorrow morning. You will have to come back and give her a description, so she can make a copy of his image to circulate."

"What about going to my family?"

Isaac did not answer right away, which meant she was not going to like his answer. "Here's the deal, Lizzy. I want to take you there, but I also want to offer you police protection."

"That will not happen, Isaac. My uncle will never agree to that."

Irritation flashed across his face and then vanished. Had she imagined it? She didn't think so. Something she had said had bothered him. A lot.

"What was that expression for?"

Rubbing his hand through his hair, he avoided her eyes for a few seconds.

"Isaac?"

Finally, he answered. "I'm sorry, Lizzy. Your safety is important. So is that of your family. I really think you should stay in town tonight where we can guard you. I can have someone go to your relatives' house and explain where you are."

That was not what she wanted. Part of her wanted to stubbornly insist he drive her out to Addie's house. But she would never forgive herself if her cousin or her other relatives were injured because of her.

"*Jah.* I would appreciate that."

His jaw dropped open. "I was sure you'd argue with me."

The shock on his face amused her. She huffed out a quiet laugh. Her amusement didn't last. "I have been in a similar situation before, Isaac. I know that sometimes it is best to work with the police."

He went still. Why had she said anything? She never talked about what had happened.

Ryder entered the room a minute later, putting their conversation on hold. Lizzy took one look at his face and knew that the news had just gone from bad to worse. Isaac straightened away from the wall and faced his coworker.

"What's the bad news?" Isaac said.

Ryder sat down at the table and stretched his long legs out in front of him.

"The bad news is that I wasn't able to get any identification on the logo. The shooter, however, might have been a different story. Did he have a scar on his forehead?" Ryder used his finger to imitate the jagged shape of the scar on his own forehead.

Lizzy started. She had forgotten about that. "*Jah.* He had a scar. It was red still, as if it were recent."

He nodded. "My sources said the shooter could be a

young man by the name of Zave. No last name. He has a rep for being a drug dealer, and a vicious one at that. Apparently, Zave has a nasty temper."

"Zave? That's unusual," Isaac mused. "Anything else?"

Ryder shook his head. "No one wanted to talk. I was astonished to get this much. Whatever he looks like, he has people scared. The word on the street is that his enemies, those who get in his way, they tend to disappear."

"A drug dealer!" Lizzy covered her mouth with her hand, horrified. The idea had never occurred to her.

Both men shot glances her way.

"It makes sense."

"What does?" she asked Isaac, even as Ryder nodded in agreement.

Isaac met her gaze squarely. "It makes sense that Zave would be a drug dealer. I think we'll find that Bill was one of his customers."

Lizzy hadn't thought the day could get much worse. She was wrong. She had fallen on the bad side of a drug dealer who had no last name, that no one could describe, but who had enough power to make people disappear.

People like her. Who was she, after all, but an Amish girl from a very small community in a quiet part of Pennsylvania? If she disappeared, would her family go to the police? It was a possibility, especially since her kidnapping. She recalled her father had allowed police officers at her brother's wedding four years ago because Rebecca had been in danger again.

They hadn't been so quick to go to the police the first time her sister had been taken, though. She re-

membered when Rebecca had been kidnapped with a
few of her school friends so many years ago. Her parents had been hesitant to work with the police, but they
had. To an extent. When it came to having Rebecca actually testify against her kidnapper, they had refused.
Rebecca had gone against her parents' and the bishop's
wishes and testified. It hadn't been a difficult decision
for her, though, because she'd already made the decision
to leave the community so she could take advantage of
the deaf community in the *Englisch* world. Being deaf
had kept Rebecca isolated from many in the community. She didn't read lips, and the language she used
was American Sign Language, which her parents had
struggled to learn. No one had blamed her when she left.

Lizzy, however, wouldn't leave.

Isaac's phone rang. He pulled it out of his pocket.
"It's the chief. Hold on a minute." He answered the
phone. "Yoder here, Chief."

It seemed strange hearing an Amish last name in
that way.

"Yes, ma'am, she's here with me. I can do that."

A second later he hung up the phone. She tensed at
the expression on his face. It was grave, and her insides
quivered as she waited to hear what was coming.

"We might have a sighting on the car that Zave drove.
It looks like he abandoned it. I didn't get a good look at
it when he drove past us, so the chief wants me to take
you to where it was found. She hopes that you might
be able to confirm it was the car used by our shooter."

She nodded. "I can do that."

He stood. "Let's head out. The sooner we find this guy, the sooner you'll be safe to go to your cousin's house."

She grabbed her cloak from the rack where it had been hanging and tossed it over her shoulders. The black bonnet was quickly pulled on over her *kapp*. Then she was ready to leave. Even as she walked out to his cruiser with him, though, Lizzy couldn't completely quell her nerves. She was once again mixed up with a killer. Would she be alive when it was all over?

FOUR

Lizzy clasped her shaking hands together on her lap, more to keep them still than for any other reason. The urge to fidget was strong but she focused on not giving in. Her father had admonished her frequently for her inability to be still. Anxiety crawled up and down her arms. She knew if she moved her cloak aside and looked down at her arms, she would see that the hairs covering them would be standing on end. She could feel the tingle.

Other than several sidelong glances, Isaac didn't seem to notice anything out of the ordinary. And why should he? He didn't know that she was prone to panic attacks. Or had been. He had no idea how hard it was for her to calmly sit next to a strange man, even a police officer. Although the fact that he was a police officer did not automatically gain her trust.

She was going to jump out of her skin soon if they didn't talk. But what could she possibly say to this strange man? She recalled the words he'd said earlier, and the slight accent of his voice, very faint, but she still detected it.

"Were you Plain before you were a cop?" The words blurted from her tongue, followed by a blaze of embarrassed warmth that slashed across her face. She couldn't believe she had asked such a personal question! Even if he used to be Amish, he might have been shunned, or left for painful reasons. Reasons that he might not want to discuss with someone he had just met.

"I'm sorry!" She met his hooded glance, saw the caution and felt even worse. "I should not have asked. It's just that I am feeling very antsy. Talking might help."

Not to mention the fact that she was very curious. Her *mamm* would definitely not approve of her asking such an intimate question. She opened her mouth to change the subject, but he was speaking before she could get anything out.

"I will say that I was Amish, growing up. I left seven years ago, when I was seventeen." His tone, while not cold, did not encourage further questions.

He left the Amish when he was seventeen. Some of her tension eased. If he had left so young, chances were that he had left before being baptized. That would have been an awkward discussion.

"I have a sister who left around the same age," she offered, wanting to show that she wasn't trying to judge him. "Rebecca is deaf, and she felt that she needed to be able to take advantage of some of the services available in the *Englisch* world. She's married to a cop from LaMar Pond, a man by the name of Miles Olsen."

"Sergeant Olsen?" Surprise colored his voice as he cast a querying glance her way.

"You know him?" Obviously, he had heard of him. Otherwise, he wouldn't know the name. She felt silly for asking.

"Sure do. We have talked a time or two at trainings and met at conferences. I have seen his wife, too. I never realized that she was former Amish like me."

Somehow, the fact that he knew Miles made her feel more comfortable around him. It was odd. Usually when she met a strange man, it took weeks of knowing the person for her be able to have a reasonable conversation. Other than worrying that she might offend him, she hadn't felt uncomfortable with being in Isaac's presence so far. She relaxed back against the seat and unclasped her hands. She stretched her fingers. They had started to ache.

Isaac steered the cruiser off the main highway, and several minutes later they were headed down a narrow dirt road. The road was similar to the one that Lizzy lived on. It was higher in the center, telling her the grader had recently been through with more gravel to level out the potholes that formed several times a year. Potholes that could damage a horse if the animal stepped into them while pulling a buggy.

The tension that had fled came back a few minutes later when Isaac pulled in behind the car that had been abandoned along the edge of the road. She could not be positive, but it looked very similar to the car driven by the man she'd seen shoot her friend's brother. So many cars looked the same to her, but it seemed too coincidental that they would find one abandoned so close to where the shooting had happened, and on the same day.

"Wait here."

Isaac eased his weapon off the belt at his waist and slowly climbed from the car. He held the weapon in front of him with his arms stiff, but kept the barrel pointed to the ground. His eyes never stopped scanning the area. She watched as he peered into the vehicle. First the backseat, then the front seat. Turning in a full circle, he scanned the area around them. Finally, she saw his posture resume its normal stance. He jogged over to where she was waiting. His short blond hair bounced on his forehead. It was endearing.

"Is this it?"

"I think so. It looks the same," she responded. That apparently was all he needed to know. He strode back to the driver's side door of the abandoned car, pulling a pair of gloves out of his pocket and putting them on before opening the front door of the vehicle. She knew that Miles carried gloves in his pocket, as well, just in case he needed to touch something in a crime scene without contaminating it. She leaned forward as he opened the door.

Nothing happened. He reached in and did something, and a second later she heard a loud clunk. The trunk bounced open an inch.

Curious, she leaned forward, watching as he hefted the trunk lid open. His whole body stilled. She knew by the abruptness that he had found something unpleasant. His one hand went to the radio on his shoulder, the other one held his weapon aloft again. He turned in a slow circle.

Her stomach churned. When he looked at her, the color leeched from her face at the stare he leveled at her. She knew that he had found something that would impact her. When he released the button on his radio and headed her way, she instinctively pushed herself back against the seat. Whatever he was going to tell her, she definitely did not want to hear it.

Isaac reached her door and opened it. He squatted down so that his face was only slightly below hers.

"Lizzy. I found a body in the trunk. From your description, I have to believe it's Bill. I will need you to confirm it."

Tears sprang to the back of her eyes. She hadn't known Bill long, and she definitely had not trusted him. She had been furious with him mere hours before now. But she certainly had not wished him to come to harm. What would she say when she saw Sue?

The fears that had started to fade to the background rushed in on her again. The last thing she wanted to do was go and look at a body. A lead ball sank to the pit of her stomach. She couldn't do it. But she knew she had to. She owed it to Sue to confirm that Bill was dead.

Casting a glance at the policeman sitting so close to her, she let the concern on his face anchor her. Isaac would be with her. She would not have to do this difficult duty on her own. Pulling a breath deep into her lungs, she held it a moment and then let it out slowly.

She started to get out of the car.

"You don't have to do it now. We can…"

She brushed his hands aside and moved to the back of the other vehicle. Holding her breath, she blinked as a form came into focus as she neared it. Gradually, the whole person came into view. She saw the ordinary face. It was so pale his skin looked like it was wax. She saw the leather jacket. The dark stain on his T-shirt. Momentarily she felt woozy when she saw it, knowing it was blood.

Tears filled her eyes. She swallowed and backed away from the trunk. Isaac's hand touched her shoulder briefly to steady her. She barely noticed. Any hope that Bill was still alive faded as she faced the undeniable proof that he had been killed.

And she was the only person who could identify his killer.

Isaac led Lizzy back to his car. Keeping his eyes locked on her face, he backed away from the vehicle and quickly called in to the station, asking when the other officer he'd requested upon finding the body would arrive. He disconnected after learning the second officer was en route. Their station had a policy to have two officers deal with a crime scene whenever possible. He scanned the Amish woman sitting in his car. She looked so small sitting there alone. All color had fled from her face. She was so pale he half expected her to pass out at any instant. He had not intended for her to see the body then, before others had arrived, but it was too late to change the fact that she had seen it. He knew how shocking that could be, especially the first time.

The first dead body he had seen had been his own

brother. He gave his head a hard shake to dislodge the thought. He had to focus on the job at hand, and on the witness sitting in his vehicle.

"Lizzy," he began. He stopped when her gaze lifted to his. The breath stalled in his body at the haunted expression mired in the blue eyes. Was she even seeing him standing before her?

"It's happening again." Her words were so soft he barely caught them.

He leaned closer to hear her. He recalled her earlier words about being in a similar situation before. It was about time he found out exactly what had happened.

"What's happening again?"

She continued to look through him. It was almost as though she had forgotten where she was or that he was there with her. He thought for a moment that she hadn't even registered his question. He was relieved when she opened her mouth to answer him, but her answer was absolutely not what he had expected.

"A little over thirteen years ago," she began, "my older sister, Rebecca, and some of her friends were kidnapped. I was never sure of all the details… I was only seven at the time, and my family did not discuss it openly. Rebecca has told me some of it. Apparently, the man was someone they knew from school. Rebecca went to an *Englisch* school for a while because they had a deaf classroom. I don't know any of the other girls involved. I know that one of the girls had died, but then the kidnapper was sent to prison and life went on. But it wasn't over. Around four years ago, we were forced to go through the situation again when his brother came after Rebecca. I was with her and he abducted us both. I will never in my life forget being chained up in that basement, just waiting to die. It was then that I really understood the concept of our mortality."

He was completely shocked by what she had admitted to him. Her voice, though quiet, was steady. She could have been discussing what she had eaten for breakfast rather than one of the most horrific experiences a person could endure. His admiration for her grew. It took strength to come out of a terrifying situation and keep your faith, but she obviously had.

"What happened? How did you get out?" he asked her, keeping his voice calm as if he were speaking to a young child and not a mature woman around his own age.

A slight smile parted her lips.

"Miles saved us. I thought we were going to die. It took me a long time to be able to sleep through the night again. I had panic attacks for over a year. But I thought, I really thought, that I had lived through the worst trauma I would ever have to go through. I was wrong—this is so much scarier, to see someone killed right in front of you. I don't feel like I have the strength to go through something like this again. But I don't have a choice, do I?"

He took a moment to think about how he could answer her. It was unfair that she would have to deal with such darkness twice in her life. Many people would have broken by now. She was scared; he could see the fear and anxiety battling within her. He could tell by her pale features that she was struggling to take in everything that had happened. But he could also see strength and determination in the way she held her posture erect.

Following his instincts, he reached out and gripped her hands in his. They were cool to the touch. She raised startled eyes to his face and finally focused on him. "Lizzy, I know this is bad, and I know that you are scared. I'll tell you the truth. I find these situations unsettling, too. But I will also give you my promise. I will not rest until you are safe and the man responsible for the death of Mr. Allister is in custody."

He held still as she searched his face. When she nodded, he felt the honor she'd bestowed. He doubted, after hearing her story, that she trusted people, or men, readily. That she was giving him her trust…he knew that he had to do his best to live up to that trust.

Gravel crunched. Another car was pulling up. Isaac stood, not wanting one of his fellow officers to see him holding the hands of a witness. Not that he had done anything wrong, but he felt like what had happened was personal, and others didn't need to know that detail. An ambulance pulled up and the coroner exited the passenger side of the car and headed immediately to the open trunk, the barest of nods his only greeting.

Ryder stepped from his own cruiser, raising a questioning eyebrow in Isaac's direction. Isaac caught the nod tossed toward Lizzy. He understood the question.

"Body in the trunk," he murmured when he was within earshot of his friend and colleague. "She confirmed that it's William Allister."

Ryder sighed and nodded. "I had hoped that we

would find that he hadn't been killed. She said he had a sister, right? Do we know if that was his only family?"

Isaac shrugged. "Guess we'll have to ask Lizzy for that information."

Lizzy, it turned out, didn't know. "I have never heard Sue talk of any other family members before. She only talked about her brother. I have no idea if there is anyone else."

Isaac exchanged a quick glance with Ryder. "Are you certain that Bill was her brother?"

"*Jah.* I was unhappy when he showed up at my house instead of Sue. She had sent a letter, but I still had him use his phone to call her. She told me she had sent him in her place because she was sick."

"No doubt he set up his meeting with Zave after he found out where he was heading."

The coroner joined them. "I will, of course, need to examine the body more thoroughly, but I feel confident in saying that the young man was killed by a single gunshot."

"We have a bullet from the scene," Ryder said.

Isaac nodded. "And the car our witness was driving might have a second bullet. So we should be able to identify the gun the bullets came from."

Isaac felt like he was replaying the scene from earlier as a tow truck came and the driver loaded up the car. Ryder stuck around long enough to see that the car was gone, then he waved and jogged back to his own vehicle. He made a U-turn in the middle of the road and soon was headed back to town.

"I need to call Sue," Lizzy said suddenly into the silence as Isaac started to drive again.

"Do you know the number?" Isaac reached into his pocket and pulled out his phone. She started to dial as soon as he handed it her. He was surprised. He had half expected her to refuse to use the phone, because the Amish didn't usually use cell phones.

"I would not use this phone, except that it is an emergency. My bishop once told me that there are times when mercy needs to take precedence over rules." She put the phone to her ear. He heard a voice answer and saw the wince cross his passenger's face. He wanted to wince in sympathy. He'd made plenty of those calls in his life.

"Sue, it's Lizzy... I'm sorry, I have bad news... No, no. I'm not hurt, but I have something to tell you about Bill."

Her voice trembled as she told Sue of the fate her brother had suffered. He could hear the moment the weeping began on the other end of the line.

"I'm helping the police, Sue. I got a good look at the shooter."

Isaac straightened in his seat. This was not information he wanted to get out to the public.

"Put it on speaker," he told Lizzy.

"Just a minute," she told the woman on the other end. Then she pulled the phone away from her ear and hit the speaker button.

"Ms. Allister? This is Officer Yoder from the Waylan Grove Police Department."

A sob echoed down the line. "Is it true? Is my little brother really dead?"

"Yes, I'm sorry. Ma'am, Miss Miller has already identified the body."

What ensued was a very painful conversation. But he got what he needed. She promised to send him a list of all her brother's known associates. Sue also assured him that she would be available tomorrow morning for a visit from the police. Hopefully, she would agree to let them search through her brother's belongings. Often a search was all that was needed to get the information necessary to tie the investigation up neatly.

It was late by the time they returned to the station.

Stifling a yawn, Isaac waved an arm for Lizzy to precede him into the office he shared with the other officers. He had stopped and picked up a quick pizza and some iced tea on the way in. Lizzy had insisted she was fine.

"You might be fine, but my stomach is feeling hollow right now. I plan on eating, and I wouldn't mind if you ate something yourself."

It turned out, he didn't need to do any more persuading. She ate her fair share of the pizza, and Ryder zoomed in to snag two slices, as well.

"We gotta put you somewhere for the night." Isaac took a long swig of iced tea. "We have our visual artist coming in tomorrow morning to work with you, so we might get a good image to send out to the nearby precincts."

"Cancel that plan, Isaac."

Isaac turned at Chief Carson's voice. Sheila Carson

was holding a bottle of water in one capable hand and her phone in the other. She looked far too young to have the responsibilities of being the chief of police, but her officers trusted her without hesitation.

"Chief?"

She indicated her phone. "I just got off the phone with the visual artist. She can't make it. Their town is under a flash flood warning, and occupants are being evacuated to higher ground. It's probably going to be at least three days before she can get here."

FIVE

Three days?

Lizzy stared at the elegant woman standing before her in dismay. She couldn't be stranded here for three days. Three days sounded like an awful long time. And what would happen to the investigation? Would her not being able to work with an artist hinder the officers' ability to search for the killer?

The tall, dark-haired chief was watching her reaction, sympathy stamped on her face. But not softness. No, this chief would not be swayed by emotional pleas.

Her sister, Rebecca, was an artist. She remembered that Rebecca had drawn such sketches for the LaMar Pond Police Department before. Of course, Rebecca was unavailable at the moment as she and her husband were out of town. She was expected back in a few days, but by then, it might be too late.

She would have to suffer through it as best she could. But where would she stay?

"Will I sleep here?" she asked the question to anyone who could answer her.

At this, the chief smiled. It was gone quickly, but it had been a smile. "No, I don't think that would work out. I have secured a room at the local motel for you. I have also made plans for guards to be posted outside the motel. You should be able to get a few hours of sleep, then we can decide how to proceed in the morning."

"Chief," Isaac said, getting his boss's attention. "I have made arrangements for a couple of local cops to go and visit the victim's sister in the morning. If they can get some information from her, it might be possible to get the answers we need without the artist."

She nodded, her dark eyes snapping with approval. "Excellent. Please keep me informed."

Lizzy found herself again under scrutiny. "Miss Miller, when you have completed your meal, maybe one of my officers could escort you to the motel. No offense, but you look worn out."

For an instant, panic started to rise inside her. The only officers she knew were Isaac and Ryder. The idea of being alone with any of the other men was enough to make her break out into a cold sweat. She didn't know that she had any choice, though. She was several hours from home and didn't know anyone else.

"If I may, Chief, I think it would be best if I drove her over."

Lizzy felt the fear subside a bit at Isaac's words. Then she chided herself. She couldn't depend on him. Despite the fact that he used to be Amish, she still didn't know him very well. Plus, he had other duties to take care of than keeping track of her. He had been very helpful, but that was because it was part of his job. Cutting her eyes at him, she bit her lip. He had to be exhausted. And she knew he had a full day planned in the morning, all of which would center around this case she was involved in. She could not, would not, expect more from him than that.

Forcing a smile she didn't feel on her face, she shook her head. He didn't look convinced. His brows drew in, and he frowned at her. "It will be fine, Isaac. I will go with the other officers."

He gave her a narrow glance. "Are you sure about that, Lizzy? I don't mind. If I can't, then I'm sure Ryder would agree to go with you."

She caught the look he threw his colleague. Ryder was silently being told that he needed to agree or else. The sweetness of it warmed her. She appreciated the care he was extending to her.

No, she would not let her guard down. It was time she remembered that she was a strong woman, even when she didn't feel that way. She could do anything with Christ at her side. Silently praying to God for strength, she smiled again.

"*Jah*, I am sure. You do what you need to do, and I will see you in the morning."

He nodded but was clearly not completely satisfied with the situation. Well, neither was she, but she couldn't think of any other way out of it.

You could go home.

She could. She knew that if she was truly in danger, her cousin would not begrudge her the decision to flee back to the safety of LaMar Pond. It was very tempting. She could almost feel the security of her parents' home surrounding her and keeping her safe. *Mamm* and *Dat* wouldn't question her if she returned home.

Except there was no guarantee that she would be safe. The man who shot Bill had obviously known him, which meant he might know where Bill lived. How hard would it really be for him to track her down? Was it possible that she could put her family in danger if she went home? That was not an option.

Another voice whispered in her mind. If she went home, she would be letting her parents protect her again. For a long time, she had been fine with that. But suddenly, she wanted more than to always be shielded from the darkness in the world. She had personally touched the darkness and had survived. God had proved that He was with her. Turning her back and running home would be nothing less than saying she didn't trust Him to care for her outside of her parents' dwelling.

By the time Isaac presented the two officers she would be going with, Lizzy had firmed her determination to see this thing through to whatever end it had. Still, she was happy to note that one of the officers was a woman. She could do this, she whispered to herself. She would protect her family, and she would help to bring Bill's killer to justice. Then she would return home to the life she was meant to lead. It would be a lonely life, but she would accept that.

Isaac walked her outside to the cruiser that would bring her to the hotel. He handed her a small cell phone. "I know that you do not use a cell phone normally. This has only one setting. It is for 911 calls only. If anything happens, use it. You can tell the dispatcher to page me directly."

She hesitated. She had used his cell phone before to call Sue, but that had been to help someone else. She felt strange taking a phone to use for her own advantage. Would it be breaking the rules? They had a phone in their business for emergencies. They had a community phone for emergencies. This was not her phone. And it was only set for emergencies. Discreetly, she slipped it into her apron, but she wondered if she would be able to use it if there ever was an emergency.

"That's my girl. Look, I will be by in the morning. Then we'll try to figure this out. I won't forget my promise to you, Lizzy. Got that?"

Her heart melted. His promise to protect her and to see that justice was done. She believed him, too. She wasn't sure how it had happened, but something about Isaac Yoder had reached out and broken through the wall of distrust and cynicism she had built up.

The fact that she was beginning to trust the earnest young man before her terrified her.

She could not afford to let any man close to her, especially not one who seemed to understand her so well. Whatever charms Isaac Yoder possessed, no matter how charming or upright he was, he was a man who had chosen to leave the Amish world. So even in the unlikely circumstance that Lizzy decided to one day marry, he would never be a choice she'd be able to make.

"I will be fine. You don't need to worry about me."

Deliberately, she got into the cruiser and turned her face forward. The car started advancing. She could feel his gaze on her as the distance between them increased. It took all her will, but she never glanced back.

Isaac gave up trying to sleep when he woke up for the third time at four in the morning. In his mind, he kept thinking about all the pieces of the puzzle, trying to figure out the best way to keep Lizzy safe.

One thing that didn't sit well was having other officers guarding her. Which was ridiculous. Isaac had known both Jill and Keith for years. They were dedicated cops who would put their lives on the line for any civilian without a second thought. Surely, they were more experienced than he was. He'd only been on the force for two years; Jill had been in for four years and Keith for close to six. He had no reason to be uneasy.

Which was easy enough to say, but in practice, it was nigh on impossible.

Heaving a sigh, he shoved the blankets aside and got up, deciding he could put the time to better use in the office. After he had dressed and shaved, he grabbed a quick breakfast of peanut butter toast, chugged a glass of ice-cold milk, brushed his teeth and gathered up his keys and his wallet.

He turned to leave the apartment, but stopped for a moment to take in the place. It felt as though he were seeing it with fresh eyes. He had lived in this apartment for the past five years. In all that time, he hadn't managed to make it feel like a home. There was nothing really personal about the place that said, "Isaac Yoder lives here." He frowned. There weren't even any paintings on the wall, or any bric-a-brac of any kind.

His mind flashed back to his home growing up. There were no pictures on the walls, but their house had definitely had personality. He could visualize the handmade rocking chair his father had made, and the china dishes in their curio cabinet. His mother had always been a quilter, and several quilts were spread throughout the house, bright with colors and intricate patterns. People thought that being Plain meant that the Amish had nothing of beauty, but that wasn't true. Beauty had been all around them in nature and in the things they had made with their hands.

But this apartment held nothing of beauty, or unique. Anyone could have lived here.

Why had he never noticed that before? More importantly, what had changed that he was noticing it now?

A pretty face with vivid blue eyes and golden blond hair peeping out from beneath a starched white prayer *kapp* popped into his mind. No way. He wasn't having that. Isaac knew that had he remained Amish Lizzy would have definitely captured his attention. However, the Plain life was something he had left years ago. He had shaken it off like a dog shakes off water after wading in the creek. He wasn't going back. He couldn't go back. There was no way to reconcile with his *dat*.

Plus, he hadn't stuck close to God when he had left. He was ashamed of that. But it had been so long since he had allowed God to guide his path he wasn't even sure how to begin to mend that relationship.

Troubled, Isaac shut the door and made his way out to his truck. He shoved the uncomfortable self-examination aside so he could focus on the case at hand.

By the time he entered the station at 4:45, he had made a mental list of the tasks he needed to get done that morning. He poured himself strong coffee—black, of course—and brought the steaming mug back to his desk to begin ticking items off his list one by one.

At eight-thirty, his phone rang, jolting him out of his concentration. His first thought was that something had happened to Lizzy. His glance shot to his pager. No, if she had called 911, or if one of the officers on duty there had done so, he would have been notified.

This was one instance in which silence was a good thing.

Blowing out a hard breath, he reached for his phone, striving to project a calmness that was only partially faked.

"Officer Yoder," he greeted the caller.

"Morning, Officer Yoder," a feminine voice responded. "This is Sergeant Claire Zerosky from the LaMar Pond Police Department. I'm afraid I have some bad news for you."

Isaac heard "LaMar Pond" and sat up straighter in his chair. The police were going to interview Sue Allister at eight this morning. The coffee in his stomach immediately transformed into a ball of heavy sludge.

"You went to see Ms. Allister?" he guessed, even though he knew there was no other reason for that particular department to be calling.

"We went out. When we arrived, her door had been breached, and the entire place had been tossed."

"And the woman?" He held his breath.

"There was no sign of her, but it sure looked like

there had been a massive struggle inside the place. There was some blood found on the kitchen floor. We will be conducting a thorough search for her, but I thought you should know. It appears that your killer is going after others who might be able to recognize him."

Lizzy!

He shot up out of his seat so fast that he upended his coffee mug, spilling the last few drops on the surface. He barely noticed it. He got off the phone with Claire Zerosky as fast as he could manage and then he was out of the station and running to his cruiser. On the way to the hotel, he called in to Chief Carson and left her a voice mail message, informing her of the latest development. Then he phoned Ryder, who rapidly agreed to meet him at the motel. His friend lived closer to the motel than the station, so they arrived at nearly the same time.

The two officers on duty jumped to attention as they saw the two cruisers zip into the lot. Lizzy was in a street-level room. He was familiar enough with this motel to know that each room was complete with a doorknob lock, a sliding chain lock and a dead bolt. How many of those locks had Lizzy employed? He knew that it was common for people in rural townships to leave doors unlocked at night. His own family had done so often.

"Report!" Isaac barked, not even caring that both Jill and Keith were the same rank as he was. His only concern was the lovely woman resting, hopefully peacefully, within the room they were guarding.

"Nothing to report, Isaac," Keith responded. "She

went in there as soon as we arrived, and hasn't come out since."

"Wait," Jill interrupted. "She asked me to order her some oatmeal for breakfast, and it was delivered fifteen minutes ago."

So she was awake and well. He huffed out a breath, puffing his cheeks out. He really needed to calm down.

"Thanks, guys. Sorry for the tone. We had some disturbing news this morning."

His colleagues shrugged it off. They'd all had their moments. He stepped past them and rapped his knuckles sharply against the door. "Lizzy, it's Isaac. I need to speak with you."

There was no sound within the room.

His skin crawled with trepidation. His mind told him he was overreacting, but his instincts screamed at him that she was in trouble. He knocked again and raised his voice. "Lizzy? Please answer the door."

Still no answer.

"Something's not right."

Keith held out an arm. "Don't get excited, Isaac. She's probably in the bathroom."

Why on earth weren't they taking this seriously? Was it because Waylan Grove was such a quiet place? Whatever the reason, he was not happy that two experienced officers were taking the current circumstances far too casually.

"Then I will apologize for alarming her. But I am going to break in and make sure she's well."

Jill rolled her eyes. Ryder took her to task for it. "Look, the only other person who could identify the perp was apparently kidnapped, possibly worse. Our guy is vicious, and the woman in there has seen him up close and personal. We're breaking down the door."

And they did.

The instant the locks broke, splintering the wood of the doorframe, Isaac was through the door, Ryder behind him. His blood froze when he crossed the threshold. Lizzy was lying still on the floor, a bowl that had apparently been filled with oatmeal shattered beside her. Gobs of oatmeal splattered the floor and the wall. Isaac ignored the gooey mess and knelt beside her. His trembling fingers felt her throat for a pulse. It was thready, but he found one. Bending closer, a faint breath hit his cheek. She was breathing. He was aware of Ryder calling 911 in the background, but kept his attention focused squarely on the unconscious woman on the floor.

"*Denke*, Jesus." The German word slipped past his lips without thought. He said another prayer that she would hold on until the paramedics arrived.

Behind him, he could hear Ryder shouting into the phone.

His glance fell on the oatmeal. An awful suspicion hit him.

She'd been poisoned. How had the killer found her? And how had he known that she had ordered oatmeal?

Jill and Keith knelt on the other side of her, both of their faces pale and shocked.

"Isaac, she was fine fifteen minutes ago. Honest. And we didn't let anyone in."

He shook his head. "You didn't need to. If I'm right,

this oatmeal was poisoned." He lifted his gaze from her for just a moment. "Who delivered the breakfast?"

Keith looked uneasy. "The woman at the front desk brought it to us. She said a delivery boy had dropped it off."

Isaac processed that information. That was strange. It was a motel, so the door was on the outside. Although the woman at the front desk might not have questioned it; many people would have hesitated to approach a room guarded by the police.

"Keith, once the paramedics arrive, you'll need to go and see if she could give a description of the delivery boy." He hated to be pessimistic, but he really didn't think their killer would be clumsy enough to allow himself to be recognized by a desk clerk. He was determined to follow every possible lead.

He looked back at Lizzy. He knew he couldn't have done anything, but he felt as though he had failed her.

He stayed on his knees by her side, keeping track of her pulse and her breathing. Had she realized what was happening? Why hadn't she used the phone he had given her? He remained where he was until the paramedics arrived five minutes later. Only then did he relinquish his place to the men who entered the room. When he mentioned his suspicion, the oatmeal and her orange juice were both saved to be transported to the hospital to be tested.

Watching the crew lift her onto the stretcher and roll it out to the ambulance, Isaac needed to do something. He went to the table and looked for the bag that the breakfast was delivered in. It was from a small diner a mile down the road. Calling Ryder over, he walked swiftly to his car. Behind him, Ryder's long stride followed.

"We need to check out Gertie's Diner. That's where the food came from."

"Sounds like a plan."

He drove to the diner, praying the whole way that Lizzy would recover. He also prayed, for the first time in a long time, that God would guide and assist their investigation. Whoever had tried to poison Lizzy was still out there. He'd already killed a man, and Sue was still missing.

It was only a matter of time before he struck again.

SIX

The owner of the diner was a small round man named Clyde.

"Sure, I remember that order. I thought it was sweet. Who orders plain oatmeal anymore? I cooked it up and sent it with Sid, one of our busboys. He was supposed to deliver it and come right back."

"Let me guess." Isaac raised his eyebrows. "Sid never came back."

"That's it exactly. I can't understand it. Sid is my best worker. He's been here for two years and has never missed a day or been late. He's like a clock. I don't mind saying, I'm concerned."

That made two of them, Isaac thought.

"Clyde, can you describe Sid for me? Is he dark-haired with a scar on his forehead?"

"Sid?" Clyde shook his head. "Nah. Red as anything, and no scars, although he does have some acne. He's only seventeen."

With a sick feeling, Isaac took down Sid's address and next of kin information. Isaac thanked the man and left the diner. He hoped that they would find Sid alive and well, but he knew in his gut that Zave, or whoever their shooter was, had most likely done something to him and had delivered the poisoned oatmeal himself. He frowned.

"I think our killer did something to Sid," he commented to Ryder, thinking out loud in an attempt to get his thoughts in order. "What I can't see is him delivering the food himself. We had clearly noted in our description that the perp had a recent scar on his forehead."

Ryder pursed his lips. "I agree. Which leads me to believe that he wasn't working alone."

Isaac called Jill. "What did the delivery boy look like?"

Jill responded instantly. "He was young. Dark hair. Beret and uniform on. Glasses."

"Was there a scar on his forehead?"

Silence. "You're thinking it was that Zave character. Honestly, the motel employee didn't say she saw a scar. But as a woman, I can tell you that many scars are easy enough to disguise with cosmetics."

Great. So they had a man who knew how to disguise himself. Their next stop was Sid's home. It was difficult to not alarm his mother. After all, her son was missing, and a known killer had taken his identity. He didn't relay all that information. When they knew for sure what had happened to the boy they would inform her. There was still the very slight possibility that Sid was fine.

Isaac did not have much faith about that being the case. He fully expected them to locate Sid's body.

The Waylan Grove Police Department gathered every available person to search for Sid. He hadn't been missing long, but he was definitely considered to be in serious danger. The search lasted through the day. The local dive team was called in to search the nearby pond and the creek bordering the town. Isaac scowled at the spectators lining the banks, craning their necks to get a glimpse of team members coming up from their search.

Isaac saw that one of the divers was emerging from the water. Pushing himself through the crowd, Isaac ignored the grumbles of the onlookers he shoved past. Grumbles which died out as he passed. People didn't want to argue with a man in a police uniform, he figured.

The diver had something. Not a body, but a backpack. The water streamed from the bottom of the pack. No doubt whatever was inside was drenched, probably ruined. He stepped closer to see what the woman had found.

Olivia Bayle glanced his way with a nod of recognition. She might have been the youngest member on the team, but he knew that she took her work very seriously. The woman was highly dedicated, and just as ambitious. She brought the backpack over to where her team had assembled their base. The backpack was systematically unpacked, a digital photo taken of each item before it was placed in plastic evidence bags to be sent in for further analysis.

One item brought out was a very soggy wallet. Olivia's gloved hands remained steady as she opened it and pulled out the driver's license.

Isaac leaned in and saw the image of a smiling young man. Sid.

"That's the kid we're looking for," he murmured. She nodded.

"We have his backpack. But there was no sign of him in the water." Olivia dropped the wallet and the license into an evidence bag. "So the question is, how did the backpack get into the water?"

"Exactly." Isaac rubbed his chin in thought. "And where's the kid?"

Those were questions they could not answer at this point.

"I wonder if Sid was a victim, as we had originally thought, or was he complicit with Zave?"

"We'll keep looking for him," Ryder stated, still eyeing the bag as if he could glean answers from it if he stared long enough.

When the sun started to set, the fatigued volunteers and search crews disbanded.

"Isaac," Chief Carson said, appearing beside him. "Do you think your dogs are ready to be used in a search?"

Isaac had become fascinated with the use of dogs in police work. He'd been given the go-ahead to become certified as a trainer and had three pups he was helping to train.

"I think one of them might be ready." It was hard to keep the sudden thrill that flooded his system from showing in his voice. This was a serious event, and he didn't want to let his enthusiasm for his dogs overshadow the very real problem of a missing teen.

"Excellent." A small lift of her lips that barely passed for a smile appeared and was gone. "We'll start the search at seven tomorrow morning."

There was nothing left he could do here. Isaac looked at the watch on his wrist. Visiting hours at the hospital would be over in a little more than an hour. Had Lizzy woken up? He'd had no word on her condition. Antsy to get to the hospital, Isaac told Ryder where he was heading, then he took off.

He walked into the hospital and couldn't stop himself from rolling his shoulders beneath his jacket. Hospitals gave him the creeps. He had never been inside one before Joshua had been left for dead by the *Englischers* who had tormented him. Isaac knew that the doctors and medical staff had done everything in their power to keep Joshua alive. Maybe they would have succeeded if the boys had only used their fists. When the drunken youths had run him over with their car, however, he'd been injured too severely for modern medicine. Isaac could never enter a hospital without the memories flooding his mind, and so he had never gotten over his feeling of distaste for the places. Still, he wouldn't let his past experiences keep him from doing his duty.

Or from seeing the woman he had promised to protect.

First, he had to confer with the doctor.

"She needs to remain overnight. We had to pump her stomach. You were right, she had been poisoned. Fortunately for her, whoever poisoned her used a very small dose."

"Will there be any long-term effects?" Isaac shoved

his curled fists into his pockets. He couldn't get the image of Lizzy lying pale and still out of his mind.

"There shouldn't be. She may find that her stomach is tender for the next few days. Also, she may have a lingering headache. An over-the-counter pain reliever should help."

"She can take medicine after consuming poison?" He was shocked. He would have assumed that would send her into an overdose. Not that he expected Lizzy to actually take medication. The idea was surprising, though.

"We got the majority of the poison out of her system. By the time she's released, the rest of it will have run its course. So yes, she can take minimal doses of meds to ease her discomfort."

Isaac was relieved to know that she would recover. He had feared the worst, even though she was in the hospital receiving treatment.

He went up to her room. A nurse was checking her IV when he entered. She sent him a professional smile. One that extended both a welcome and a warning. He got the message.

"She's still sleeping, Officer. Rest is the best thing for her right now."

"Yes, ma'am." He felt like a kid being chastised. He almost smiled at the thought. "I'll do my best not to disturb her. I just plan on sitting here for a few moments."

The stare she leveled at him clearly indicated that she didn't trust him. He waited until she had left the room before he eased himself down into the chair next to the bedside. Her color was better, he was glad to note. It was not nearly as waxy as it had been when he had come upon her that morning. One could almost make the mistake that she was sleeping. Almost.

He sat for five minutes, just watching her. Being next to her, knowing that she would recover, he felt the peace that flowed into his soul. That gave him pause. He didn't like the fact that he was feeling protective toward her. While he was often sympathetic toward victims he worked with, he had never let it go beyond that. Something about Lizzy, though, was different.

He frowned. She was nothing more than a witness to a murder. An Amish witness. A way of life he had turned his back on forever.

It was time for him to leave. He needed to keep searching for the criminal that was after her. He was out there somewhere, and Isaac would keep looking until he could no longer harm anyone.

He shifted forward in his seat.

Lizzy sighed and stirred. Isaac halted his movement, holding his breath. Would she awaken?

Fluttering like a butterfly, her lashes slowly rose to reveal confused blue eyes.

His breath caught. She blinked. Once, twice, three times. On the third time, her eyes remained open. Her head turned, and she sought him out. The corners of her lips lifted.

His heart skittered and skipped in his chest.

He was in so much trouble.

Where was she? Why was she lying down?

Lizzy slowly fought her way out of the fuzzy cocoon she was stuck in. After a few minutes, she noticed the

IV hooked to her arm. Why was she in the hospital? A dual ache throbbed behind her eyes. She blinked to clear them. There was a window to her right. Outside, she could see that it was dark. Stars were liberally strewn across the sky, glittering like the sequins on a black velvet dress she'd seen Rebecca wear once. She frowned, wrinkling her forehead as she tried to remember what had happened.

And then she became aware of the man at her bedside.

Isaac.

Why was he here? He was staring at her like he'd never seen her before. His eyes had a new wariness to them. Something must've happened.

Wait a minute. She remembered ordering breakfast that morning. She had been eating oatmeal. It had had a funny taste to it, but she didn't notice until after she'd eaten several bites.

"I was poisoned, wasn't I?"

Her voice was rusty. She really needed a drink of water. She tried to swallow, but it didn't help.

"Thirsty."

"Wait a minute, I'll get help."

He dashed out the door. She watched him leave, then wearily shut her eyes again. She couldn't remember ever feeling so completely worn out, as if she had just run here all the way from home. Everything felt weighted down. Her legs, her arms. Even her eyelids felt like they had weights attached to them.

Distantly, she became aware of voices. Isaac had returned with a nurse. Oh, she had told him she was thirsty. At the memory, she became conscious of the raspiness in her throat.

"Well, it looks like she's fallen asleep again," a cool voice remarked.

The nurse was going to leave. She had to stop her, or who knew how long it would be until she got a drink. But opening her eyes seemed to take too much of her energy.

"Awake," she murmured, her lips slow to do what her brain commanded.

Someone took her hand and patted it in a comforting way. She dragged her eyes open. Her lids felt as if they were weighted down with cement blocks. Isaac was still standing beside her bed, shifting on his feet and looking around awkwardly.

"Here you go, dear." The nurse appeared at her other side, a cup filled with water and ice in her hands. She held the straw to Lizzy's lips. The water was cold, and it tasted so good. Lizzy took three long swallows before letting her head relax back against her pillow.

"Visiting hours end in five minutes," the nurse warned Isaac. She started to leave the room. Isaac rolled his eyes. Lizzy bit her lips to suppress the smile trying to escape. It would be rude and she didn't want to offend the woman. She was doing her job and looking out for her patient.

She sighed when the door closed behind her. "When will I be able to leave?"

"The doctor said they're keeping you tonight to make sure you're stable. I'll have someone come and pick you up in the morning."

Her stomach flipped. The water she had drank churned in her belly.

"Hey, don't look like that. I will do my best to make sure it's someone you know, or maybe a female cop. I haven't forgotten what you told me."

She didn't want it to be any other cop, regardless of whether or not they were female. Isaac was the officer that she had started to trust. He was the one she wanted to get her.

Realizing how selfish she was being, Lizzy fought to keep her disappointment hidden. Isaac had a duty to do. Being related by marriage to Miles, she knew that when police officers talked about their duty, it was not something that they took lightly.

"Has there been any progress? Do they know who poisoned me?"

It was probably the guy who had shot Bill. But how had he located her so fast? And how had he gotten past the cops? She shivered.

"Are you cold?"

Her eyes widened. She hadn't expected him to be so observant. He was waiting for her to answer him. "*Nee*. I am not cold. I am concerned that someone was able to get to me even with the police outside my door. I thought I would be safe. Wasn't that why I had to stay in that motel instead of going to see my family?"

A tide of color washed up Isaac's face, blending with his hairline. It had not been her intention to embarrass him, but she meant what she said.

"I understand your concern. I really do. I have asked the same questions. I'll be honest with you, Lizzy. I really think that Zave is the man we are looking for. I'm just not sure what his connection is with the kid from the diner."

What? This was something she hadn't heard about. Despite the overwhelming exhaustion she was experiencing, she used her hands to push herself up into a sitting position against her pillow. She needed to be alert right now.

"Mach langsamer," she said, telling him to slow down. "What kid are you talking about? I haven't heard any of this before."

She hated feeling like she was being left out of so much relevant information.

"Attention visitors: visiting hours are now over. They will resume again at eight o'clock tomorrow morning."

Isaac glanced at the clock in the corner of the room. She wasn't about to let him leave yet, though. She needed answers. She deserved answers.

"Okay, I'll tell you as much as I can, but then I have to leave. It seems that the man who poisoned you had used the identity of a young man who worked at the diner. His name is Sid, and at this moment he remains missing. We have located his backpack at the bottom of the pond. But we have yet to find Sid."

Her throat went dry, as if someone had stuffed a wad of cotton down it. She reached out and grabbed for the water the nurse had left on the nightstand and took a couple of quick swallows so she could continue asking him questions.

"Do you think he's dead?"

He hesitated. "I'm not sure. I don't know why someone would kill him and get rid of his backpack and not dispose of his body at the same time."

Tensing, Lizzy leaned forward. "What does your instinct say? Your *bauchgefühl*?"

Isaac scratched his head, slumping slightly in his chair. He looked so tired. A tender feeling welled up inside her. She had a sudden urge to reach out and push his blond bangs off his forehead. Shocked at herself, she clasped her hands tightly in her lap to make them behave. She did not have urges like that. And she didn't like it that Isaac was making her have such feelings. It didn't matter that he used to be Amish. He wasn't now, and she doubted he would ever return. Most people who left didn't return.

"My gut feeling says that he's not dead. That there is a connection between Sid and Zave," he answered. She was so rattled by her unexpected feelings that it took her a few seconds to remember what it was that she had asked him. He wasn't done. "Tomorrow, we will continue searching for the boy. But I'm also going to be trying to find that connection. I think if we find that we will have some answers."

She had so many things she wanted ask him. Unfortunately, at that moment the door swung open. The nurse surged into the room like a prison warden. Her expression was sheer steel. She pinned Isaac with a stare that said she meant business.

"Officer, you need to leave, now."

Meekly, Isaac rose to his feet and moved to the door. "Yes, Nurse." He gave Lizzy a smile over his shoulder.

"Someone will be here to pick you up as soon as the doctor releases you. I will see you sometime tomorrow."

The nurse sniffed.

A thought struck Lizzy. "What if someone tries to get to me in here?"

He was already shaking his head. "Your door will be guarded. And this time no one will get past the officers."

Then he turned and was gone.

She allowed the nurse to help her move back down until she was once more lying on her back. The blood was pounding in her ears. How would she ever manage to sleep, wondering who was outside her door? *A hospital is safer. There are guards and security procedures*, she told herself, trying to convince herself she was safe.

It didn't help. Her thoughts continued to whirl chaotically. When the nurse flipped the light switch to turn off the lights, Lizzy bit the inside of her cheek to keep from begging the woman to leave the lights on. She was no longer a frightened seventeen-year-old. She was a responsible woman. She could handle sleeping in the dark.

Voices passed her door and she felt herself tense, fear clogging her throat. The voices faded as the people in the hall continued on their way, unaware of the affect their low-voiced conversation had on her. A man laughed. She shuddered, remembering the hard chuckle of Chad Weller as he had tormented his hostages four years ago.

Lizzy pressed her face into her pillow and squeezed

her eyes shut, trying to block out both the voices and the memories.

It was going to be a long night.

SEVEN

Isaac was at the police station by 6:35 the next morning. He'd been awake since five. The intricacies of this case were making it difficult for him to separate his work from his life. Not that he had a lot going on in his personal life. He just liked to be able to keep his work confined to the time that he was actually on duty.

He couldn't do that now. Not with Lizzy in constant danger.

He flinched away from the whisper at the back of his mind that said he was letting the Amish woman get to him. He shrugged off that idea. He was doing his duty, that was all. So he was concerned about her? Who wouldn't be, given that she was stuck in such a horrible situation?

His explanation didn't quite ring true, even to his own mind.

Lily, the sweet German shepherd pup he had purchased from a breeder, nudged him with her cold wet nose. He grinned down at her and scratched her behind the ears. She could do with a trim, he mused absently.

The sharp tap of black uniform shoes caught his attention. He recognized the sound of the walk. Brisk, but not in a hurry. The sound of a person who knew exactly where they were going and what they were going to do when they got there. Three seconds later, Chief Carson strode into the large office room littered with desks. Her eyes sought out Lily. Isaac caught her smile before she was able to banish it. Chief Carson had a reputation for being serious, almost to the point of being cold. Isaac knew this wasn't the truth. He had observed her several times when she had let her guard down. He had always wondered why she strove so hard to keep herself guarded. But he would never ask. It didn't matter how many years he had been away from his Amish community. He could never rid himself of some habits, one of which was you didn't involve yourself unasked in the business of other people. No matter how curious you might be.

"Which one is this, Isaac?" the chief asked. Her fingers flexed slightly.

"This is Lily," he replied, wondering if she was holding herself back from petting the dog. "I haven't given her the command for working yet, so if you want to pet her, you may."

It was one of the first things he learned. You did not pet or play with the dog while they were working. Once they were released from work, however, you could pet them and play with them as much as you wanted.

Chief Carson shook her head and folded her hands across her chest. "We need to get the search under way."

Nodding, Isaac rose to his feet and fastened the leash

on Lily's harness. The dog stilled, her round brown eyes fastened on his face, ears alert. He could feel the muscles beneath the short black-and-gold fur quivering with anticipation. German shepherds were thought of as aggressive dogs, but they were also very intelligent dogs. They trained well and were reliable and loyal to their handlers. Lily had probably guessed that she was going to be put to work.

"You're the only one trained to work with her, so you stick close to her today."

"Yes, Chief." This meant he definitely would not be the officer picking up Lizzy when she was released from the hospital later that morning. He had figured as much, but a pang of regret squeezed his heart, nonetheless. He ignored it. He had a job to do. Besides, he knew that Jill was familiar with Lizzy. Plus, she and Keith both felt the need to redeem themselves after the motel fiasco. It would be a long time before either of them let down their guard while on duty again.

The chief strode toward the door.

"Hier," Isaac said softly to Lily, giving her the German command to come. The dog promptly stood and came to his side. Together they left the station. When they got to his cruiser, Lily jumped up and sat in the passenger seat, her tail thumping against the leather seat. Isaac backed out of his space and drove toward the pond. Hearing panting beside him, he flicked a quick glance to the dog sitting beside him. She looked like she was grinning, the way her mouth was open and her tongue was lolling out.

At least one of us is looking forward to what's ahead.

Because as much as he had been looking forward to seeing his dogs in use, the truth was that there might be a dead body found at the end of the day. It was never a pleasant thing to know that someone's life was over. Especially—his lips tightened—when the person was so young.

The face of a certain Amish woman filled his mind. Or when it was someone that he was trying to protect. Someone he was starting to care for.

No. He would find who was after the pretty Amish woman, and then he would step back out of her life. He would not allow himself to be drawn to her, he promised himself. To have a future with her would mean returning to the Amish life, and he could not do that. He had promised Joshua that he would make sure those who didn't have a voice had one through him. That there would be justice.

Justice that Joshua never had.

Isaac arrived at the pond and managed to snag a parking space next to the chief's car. He turned off the engine, thoughts of Joshua and Lizzy still swirling around in his head.

A knock on his window startled him.

Chief Carson was watching him, a concerned frown touching her unlined face.

Oops. He must have been sitting there caught up in his thoughts for a while. His ears grew hot. Pocketing his key, Isaac stepped from the car and quickly put on his protective gear and the helmet with the attached microphone. Then he walked around to open the door by Lily. The pup jumped down at his command.

"Do we have something with Sid's scent on it?" he asked the chief.

"Yes. His mother let us have this." She handed him a high school jacket. Three letters in basketball. One more sign that this was a kid who stuck with things, not one that fled when things got tough. Not a sign of someone who would be working with a killer.

So what had really happened to him? Isaac's gut clenched.

Leaning down, he let the dog sniff the jacket and memorize the scent.

"Voran." He gave her the German command for search.

Lily bounded away, not running, but moving fast, her nose to the ground. Isaac kept a tight hold of her leash, loping behind her. It might have been one of their practice runs, it was so familiar. Except that he knew a real person in trouble was at the other end of the search. If Sid wasn't already dead.

He forced himself to focus on Lily and the path ahead, every now and then jumping to avoid tripping on low-hanging branches or skipping to the side to miss a woodchuck hole. Lily surged forward, tugging him after her as her lope became more aggressive. She had caught Sid's scent.

Adrenaline coursed through him. They were getting close. Feet pounded behind him. The other officers in on the search were keeping up, but staying back so as not to interfere with the German shepherd's concentration. Isaac ignored them all, completely in tune with the canine leading them.

How far had they run? A mile? A mile and a half? He ran three miles every morning to keep himself in shape, and it felt like they were nearing the halfway point. Of course, the terrain was different, which made it more challenging to judge the distance.

Lily slowed near the entrance to a low cave. He had been in this area many times in the past seven years, but had never paid any attention to the opening in the rocks before. Bringing out his service weapon, he called for a flashlight in a low voice, knowing the sensitive microphone would pick it up. Someone moved to his shoulder. Ryder was there with a flashlight, poised to be the spotter as they took the operation into the cave.

Senses alert, he moved into the closed-in area. Gunfire in a cave could be a disaster. He prayed that no weapons would need to be fired in this small space.

A shuffling sound came from ahead of him. Something was there. Lily bounded ahead, barking and growling. She might have been a pup, but she sounded as fierce as any grown dog set on cornering her prey.

A male voice yelled. It was a young voice, filled with terror. Ryder swung the flashlight until the beam landed squarely on the young man trying to press himself into the stone wall to escape from the dog snarling at him.

"Lily, *fuss*." Isaac issued the command for her to stand down.

Immediately, she sat, although her muscles remained tense. He knew if he told her to attack, she was ready. A steady growl continued to emanate from her. They'd have to work on that.

"Don't shoot!" Sid begged. "I don't have a gun or anything!"

No, he didn't. He did, however, have a lot to explain. Like how he knew a man suspected of being a drug dealer and a murderer. They didn't have enough evidence to prove that Zave was guilty of these crimes, but Isaac didn't doubt they would get it. He also wondered how Zave had taken Sid's car, not to mention why his backpack with his identification had been at the bottom of the pond and why he was hiding out in the cave.

Sid may not have been dead, but right now, he wasn't looking innocent, either.

Keith and Jill escorted Lizzy inside the police station. They were very solicitous. If she had to guess, she would say they were trying to make amends for allowing her to be poisoned on their watch. She didn't hold it against them, although she didn't trust them as completely as she did Isaac.

She was not going to try to analyze that.

Jill's cell phone rang. She looked at the number on display before answering it. "Hi, Isaac. We have Lizzy at the station now."

She listened, her head bobbing in response to whatever he was saying on the other end. "Oh, hey, that's good. Glad Lily worked out… Really?"

A minute later, she pressed a button to disconnect the call.

"That was Isaac," she stated unnecessarily. "He is on his way in. They used one of his dogs and were able to find the kid."

"Nice," Keith said in a satisfied tone.

"His dog?" Lizzy was confused.

Jill chuckled. "Yeah. Our Isaac is fascinated with training dogs. He became a trainer and has been working with three young dogs for months to train them to be used in police work. He has been really anxious to try one out, and he finally got his chance this morning."

Lizzy looked between the officers. They seemed to be genuinely happy for Isaac and proud of him at the same time. In fact, Keith's expression reminded her of how her older brothers looked at her when she'd done something well. These were more than just coworkers, she realized. These were Isaac's family. He had left his community, but had found another one. It took her a moment to realize that she was feeling jealous of them that they were so close to Isaac. It shocked her. And it frightened her. She couldn't afford to develop feelings for the cop. Yes, he was handsome, and he had rescued her several times. And yes, he seemed to understand her and he didn't judge her for her ridiculous fears and anxieties. Rather, he seemed to feel that what she felt was natural and completely rational.

"Anyway," Jill continued, interrupting her thoughts. "They are bringing the kid in for questioning."

"He's alive!" Isaac's instinct had been right, Lizzy thought. "Was he involved with the man who shot Bill? Did he help to poison me?"

Jill held up her hands, halting the stream of questions. Lizzy snapped her mouth shut, although she still had plenty of questions simmering inside her, ready to boil over.

"I don't know, to both of your questions."

Lizzy's shoulders sagged. She had been hoping for some real answers. She needed to get back to her family.

"What's happening now?" Keith took a long swallow of the hot coffee he'd just poured for himself. He held up another cup toward Lizzy, offering her some coffee, too. Gratefully, she nodded. He poured a second cup, then handed it to her. "Cream or sugar?"

She shook her head. "*Nee*, thank you. I'm *gut*."

Inhaling the fragrant brew, she took a small sip. It was hot, strong and bitter. Just the way she liked it.

"To answer your question, Keith, Isaac wants us to remain here with Lizzy. He's going to bring Sid in for an interview, but he wants Lizzy to look in on the interview and see if she recognizes him." She met Lizzy's eyes, her own brown eyes warm with concern. "He doesn't think you will recognize him, but he needs to know for sure."

Twenty minutes later, Lizzy found herself wedged between the two cops, staring in through a two-way window at a young teenage boy with bright red hair, around seventeen or eighteen, sitting across from Isaac and Ryder. The poor kid looked terrified. He hardly looked like a boy capable of being part of such a horrible scheme. Chad Weller's handsome face again filled her mind. To look at him, he had not appeared to have been capable of such evil, either. Her bishop frequently said that appearances of beauty and goodness often hid darkness and ugliness.

She returned her focus to the young man being interviewed. Even knowing that beauty sometimes hid evil, she had a hard time imagining him being actively involved in what had transpired yesterday. Although, she considered, if he did have a part in what had happened to her, she supposed that he deserved to be in the position he now found himself in. Lizzy was not a vengeful person, but she did believe that people should pay their debts. And that included making amends for wrongdoings, whether done out of malice or cowardice.

The door opened and a woman entered the room. She looked like him. Brown eyes, red hair surrounding a pale face dotted with freckles. His mother. Sid saw her and his shoulders drooped. In fact, the boy's entire body sagged, like a doll that had lost its stuffing.

"Mom," he choked out.

The woman's eyes filled with tears. "Sidney." Her mouth opened like she'd say more, but the emotion wouldn't allow her to. Instead, she sat beside her son and took his hand.

"Ma'am," Ryder addressed her. "We have already read your son his rights but let me quickly go over them again."

As the officer read the rights, the woman's face grew stark. There was so much pain in those eyes Lizzy found herself blinking away her own tears.

Isaac's face was set like stone, though she did see his Adam's apple bob as he swallowed. He wasn't immune to a mother's tears, either. She was glad to see that human flaw break through the hard image he displayed now.

"Mrs. Perry, before we continue, your son has declined a lawyer. He's not eighteen yet, so it's your decision."

She looked out over the table. "He'll be eighteen in two weeks. A lawyer never did his dad no good, so for now let's just keep going. If I change my mind, I'll let you know."

Isaac opened the folder and casually withdrew a paper. He set it before Sid. The boy flinched. Lizzy realized that it was a blown-up photo that Isaac was showing him. Isaac tapped one long finger on the picture. Sid's eyes followed his finger as if transfixed.

"We got this from a traffic camera. It's not a very clear image, but I'm hoping it's clear enough for you to tell me if you know who this man is?"

Lizzy jumped a bit at Isaac's harsh tone. She had never heard him speak in any tone other than the cop's soothing voice he used with her. She was seeing another side to him right now. This was not Isaac who used to be Amish. This was Officer Isaac Yoder, a member of the Waylan Grove Police Department. There was no sign of softness in him now.

Sid apparently had no trouble recognizing the seriousness in Isaac's voice. His already pale skin grew even paler, making his freckles stand out. His red hair stood on end as if he had been running his fingers through it in agitation.

"I—I have met him before." The tremble in the boy's voice told Lizzy that he had more than just met Zave before.

"Details!" Isaac barked. Sid flinched. "I need details. I don't know if you realize how much trouble you could be in. We are looking for this man on at least one count of murder. He used your vehicle and your name to attempt a second murder. I have no doubt that the deeper we dig, the more crimes we will find attributed to him. Right now, since you are sitting across from me, unless you give me something that tells me otherwise, you might very well be charged with accessory to murder."

Mrs. Perry covered her mouth with her hand, a small sob escaping. But she didn't say anything.

"Why isn't she asking for a lawyer? It doesn't make any sense." Keith waved a hand in Mrs. Perry's direction.

Jill was looking something up on her phone. "I'm looking at the family history here. Mr. Perry was sent to jail ten years ago. He died there a year and a half ago. It seems their lawyer did nothing for them except run up the bills. Mrs. Perry had to declare bankruptcy. My guess is she has lost all faith in lawyers."

"It's a shame," Keith muttered. "If that were my son in there, he'd have had a lawyer first thing."

Jill flicked him a hooded glance, although Lizzy wasn't sure why.

Isaac and Ryder were both watching Mrs. Perry. They were waiting for her to request a lawyer, she realized. When it became obvious she wouldn't, the interview continued.

"Dude, I didn't kill nobody!" Sid abruptly sat up and put his elbows on the table. His pale face flared red, brown eyes snapping. "I got myself into some trouble earlier. I needed money fast, and a buddy hooked me up with Zave. I didn't know what he was capable of then. When it came time to pay him back, I didn't have the money. He told me he would forgive the debt, but I owed him a favor. I was so relieved not to have to pay him back I agreed. When he came back and told me he needed to borrow my car, I didn't think anything of it. If that's what he needed to pay my debt, that was fine with me. But then I was talking about it with my buddy and he said that this guy was bad news. Told me about how someone else had owed him a favor, and when the dude couldn't pay it or refused to do it, this Zave guy had him killed. I was freaked out, and then I saw the police towing my car away. I got scared. I knew my mama couldn't pay for a lawyer again. I panicked and ran. I don't think I planned to leave forever, just long enough to get my head on straight."

Sid began to cry in earnest. "He's going to hear that I talked to you and he's going to come after my family. I got a little sister to protect. She's only fourteen."

Isaac's face changed at the mention of the sister. "I'll be right back."

He shoved his chair back and stood. He strode to the door, leaving the other three people in the room staring after him.

A moment later he joined Lizzy, Keith and Jill in the hall outside the interview room. His gaze snagged Lizzy's. "Did you recognize him?"

"*Nee*, I have never seen him before. Oh, but, Isaac, my heart is breaking for him. Can you protect him and his family?"

He gave her a single nod. "That's my plan." He turned to Keith. "I need you to check on his sister. Then

I need her brought here until we can figure out what to do. This Zave guy is pure evil. We might need to put the Perrys in some kind of safe house or witness protection or something to keep this family safe. If Sid and Lizzy will both testify, we might be able to put Zave away for good."

EIGHT

Testify?

The Amish did not testify in court. She would have to get permission from her bishop to do so, and she had very strong doubts about him giving her permission. After all, he hadn't wanted Rebecca to testify against her kidnapper.

But if she didn't testify, would that mean that Zave would remain free to prey upon the innocent?

Isaac didn't give her much chance to mull over the idea before he was back in the room and continuing with the interview. She didn't pay attention to much after that. Her thoughts were consumed with what would be the right thing for her to do. What if she was asked to testify and knew her testimony would put Zave in jail for good, but her bishop denied her permission? To go against one's bishop meant to risk being shunned by the community.

A fist closed around her cold heart at the idea of being separated forever from her family. Even Rebecca, who had deliberately chosen to leave the Amish life, still had access to her family because she had never been baptized in the Amish church. But Lizzy had been baptized two years ago. There was no choice for her.

She came out of her fog to realize that Sid and his weeping mother were being led out of the interview room. As they filed past her, Sid caught sight of her. He stopped and stared before approaching where she stood.

Lizzy tensed, ready for his anger. After all, she was, in essence, the reason he was now in the police station. If Zave had not decided to go after her and try to silence her, he would never have needed to borrow the young man's car.

To her surprise, Sid did not attack her. Instead, he apologized.

"They told me an Amish woman was attacked. I'm so sorry. If I had not been so irresponsible, he wouldn't have come to me to borrow a car. I would not have been able to be used to hurt you."

"He would've just found someone else. You were just a tool he used. A man like that, he would have found a way."

Sid nodded, his face sad. "Yeah, but I still feel guilty. I've never hurt anyone in my life. I'm still not sure how this even happened."

She knew the feeling.

"Honestly, I do not believe you are responsible for any of this. But if it makes you feel better, I forgive you."

Before he could respond, the door to the office swung open. A teenage girl with long red hair, wearing a pair of shorts and a shirt advertising a high school track team, stormed into the room. Her face was streaked with tears, but she looked mad.

Uh-oh. Family drama. Lizzy felt the first desire to smile that she'd had all day. This lovely young girl didn't appear to be injured in any way. She just appeared to be offended.

"Mama, what's going on? These cops dragged me away from my track meet. Do you know what that's going to do to my reputation? I can already hear the gossips now, going on about how Angie Perry was taken out of an official meet by the cops. What's Brian going to think?"

Ryder rolled his eyes and hurriedly persuaded the small family to move into a conference room. Jill grinned and went in with them.

"Thank you," she saw Ryder mouth to the other officer. The girl, Angie, was still complaining loudly when the door closed, leaving the office in blissful silence.

Lizzy couldn't help it. She saw the look that Isaac and Ryder exchanged and snickered. She tried to cover it up as best she could. Beside her, Isaac chuckled. Soon the whole group was laughing quietly.

The laughter died too quickly.

"What's going to happen to them now?" Lizzy asked, her heart aching for the trials that were just beginning for the little family.

Isaac shrugged, his face unhappy. "I don't know, Lizzy. I wish I could tell you that everything is going to be fine. It's possible, though, that they'll have to go into witness protection. That's never easy."

Miles had once explained witness protection to her.

It sounded dreadful. No contact with anyone from your previous life. Not family or friends. If you had gained some sort of fame or notoriety for a certain hobby or skill, you had to give it up so that you wouldn't run into someone who'd recognize you from it. She thought of the girl she'd just been laughing at. Would Angie still be allowed to be on the track team?

She thought of herself at fourteen years old. How would she have felt if she had had to give up all of her friends, everything that was familiar to her, because one of her siblings had gotten into trouble? She probably would've resented that sibling. She winced in sympathy for the family. No, they would not have an easy time adjusting.

But they would be alive, and they would have a chance to build a good life.

Hopefully, it would be enough.

Isaac's phone buzzed. He looked at it and smiled. "Finally."

"You get some good news, buddy?" Ryder hooked his thumbs into his pockets and leaned back against a desk.

"Could be. They found the second bullet in Allister's car. It's a match for the one I pulled out of the wall. I'm off to check on it."

He was already on his feet and putting his jacket back on. His face was set, completely focused on getting a job done.

Did that mean she was being left here? She didn't want to be whiny, but she sure hated not having any control over what was happening. She had made a point of being in control of what happened in her life as much as possible for the past few years. But in the past three days, she'd been in a whirlwind of chaos and activity and she felt like she could not get a good grasp of anything happening around her. It made her feel unsettled and she didn't like that.

Isaac was watching her face. His eyes were sympathetic. She didn't want sympathy. She wanted control. Something she had not had a lot of in the past few days. And she was tired of it.

"Come on, Lizzy. Why don't you come with me?" Isaac's words surprised her, but she wasn't going to turn him down. She shoved her black bonnet on over her *kapp* and swung her black cloak over her shoulders.

Ryder raised his eyebrows. "You could leave her here with us. We don't bite."

Lizzy held her breath. She didn't mind Ryder so much, or even Keith. Although she felt better when Jill was with them. But she didn't want to stay. She would feel safer, and more in control, if she went with Isaac. Plus, she would have more of an idea of what was happening.

"Officer Yoder." The chief stepped forward. Lizzy bit her lip. The lovely African American woman wielded her command the way Lizzy wore her cloak. It was so familiar that she was comfortable in it. Once she donned it, she didn't even think about it anymore. "This is not normal procedure. We don't take civilians with us on investigations."

Lizzy felt her hope sink. She was going to be stuck here at the station while Isaac went about his business. She couldn't ask him to stay with her. That would be needy and rude. Suddenly it all caught up with her and she wanted to wilt with exhaustion.

Isaac pulled out a chair next to a desk. *"Hoch dich anne,"* he murmured, telling her to sit down. "I will be right back."

Gratefully, she sank down into the chair. Isaac asked the chief if he could talk with her for a moment. They went into another room. When the door shut, she saw the chief's name on a gold plate on the door. Sighing, Lizzy closed her eyes to rest while Isaac and the chief discussed her fate.

Isaac faced his chief, knowing that what he was going to ask was unusual, and that was putting it mildly. She had not been mistaken when she said that taking civilians along on investigations was an extraordinary thing to even suggest. He knew that. However, Lizzy was another case.

"Well, Isaac?" Chief Carson lifted one well-groomed eyebrow in question.

He cleared his throat. "I know it isn't normal to take someone out with us. But I have several reasons why I think I should take her with me. The first reason is that we only have two people who can identify Zave right now. One of them is a seventeen-year-old kid who will probably be going into witness protection. Fortunately, the marshals are coming in from the opposite direction of the floodwaters. The idea is that he'll be able to testify once we catch our perp."

She indicated that he should continue.

This was where he had to be double careful. He took

a deep breath and braced himself. "Lizzy is an adult who looked directly into the killer's eyes. She's very calm and contained and could easily identify him." So far, so good. All of that was true. "We are a very small police department. At the moment, we only have five police officers here. She needs to be kept under guard, that's true, but—" he hoped Lizzy would forgive him "—you should also know that I am the only officer she trusts."

"Explain that."

Isaac briefly described Lizzy's history. He'd looked up her case, and it was gruesome. When he told the chief about the young Amish woman's past trauma, he saw the sympathy spark in her gaze, while her face remained still. "She trusts me, maybe partially because she knows I was raised Amish. I believe it would be less traumatic for her to come with me. Plus, it would not be such a drain on our department. If all goes well, we will have more evidence and soon be able to make an arrest."

He waited.

She frowned at him. Never a good sign. He knew his argument was a weak one. Any of the other officers at the station would have been more than capable of watching over Lizzy while he was gone. He didn't want to leave her, though. It was that simple. For some reason, he knew that she had started to trust him. After the experience she had had, it was amazing that she trusted any strange man. He didn't want to put her in a position where she would be uncomfortable.

Then he recalled her expression when he had mentioned the possibility of her testifying. He knew exactly what had been going through her mind. He had grown up in an Amish community. He knew that asking her to testify was not something that was done.

What would happen if her testimony was needed?

He forced his attention back on his chief. He couldn't allow himself to get distracted with anything else right now. He had a killer on the loose. Whether or not Lizzy agreed to testify at some later date was irrelevant. If they couldn't find Zave, her life would always be in danger.

He would do everything in his power to protect her and bring her home to her family. His chest ached as he considered her leaving for good.

"You okay, Isaac?" The chief gave him a quizzical look. He realized he was rubbing his chest to soothe away the sudden ache.

He dropped his hand, feeling his ears grow hot. What was he doing? "Yes, Chief."

She smiled at him. He blinked in surprise. He liked the chief, and he had great respect for her personally, and for the authority she held. That being said, he could probably count on one hand the times she'd smiled at him. She was a very serious person.

"Your reasons are a bit weak, Isaac." He sighed. She was going to deny his request. "But I'm going to allow her to go with you, for reasons of my own."

He didn't know what to say. And what did she mean by reasons of her own? What possible reason could she have for wanting Lizzy to go along with him?

Whatever they were, he wasn't going to stand here and debate. He had a killer to find.

"Thank you, Chief."

Before she could change her mind, he left the office and went to find Lizzy. "The chief said you could come with me."

Immediately, she stood and followed him out of the office. "Before we leave here, I want to stop by and see our weapons expert. I'm curious to see what he has to say about the bullets we gave him."

The examiner didn't even blink at seeing Isaac arrive with Lizzy. "Glad you could come down. I looked at both of the bullets that you sent me. Check this out."

Obediently, Isaac looked. He had no idea what he was looking for.

"Now, as you know, bullets are never exactly alike, but both of these bullets have five grooves of equal width. They appear to have come from a Smith and Wesson nine-millimeter revolver."

If they could find the actual gun, the bullets could be matched to it. Thanking the examiner, they left.

"Where do we go now?" Lizzy asked. He realized she was practically running to keep up with him and slowed his stride. Ach, she was a little thing. He hadn't realized before how much taller he was than her. His protective instincts hiked up a notch.

"Well, we know the kind of gun that was used. My guess is that he didn't buy it by any legal means. I am going to ask Ryder to continue searching for the logo that was on Bill's hat. I know that the LaMar Pond police are searching for Sue. I think we will go to town and see if anyone else has seen Zave around since the poisoning. It's not likely that he stuck around, but maybe we can find something that will help us locate him."

The next few hours were absolutely exhausting. To her credit, Lizzy never complained as they talked with shop owners and business people all through the main district of Waylan Grove. Whenever Isaac would show the photo taken from the traffic camera, he was met with blank stares.

"He knew something," he said after one restaurant owner shooed them away quickly, complaining that they would drive away his customers. "Did you see how nervous he got when he saw the picture? He didn't even wait to hear anything more. He just looked around and forced us to leave. My guess is he's had dealings with our guy and is afraid of being seen talking to us."

"The way that Sid was afraid Zave would know he'd told the police about their interactions." Lizzy pursed her lips and tilted her head to look up at him. The look was so beguiling, for a moment Isaac stared at her, his heart thudding.

Realizing he hadn't responded, he gulped and looked away from her. She was far too attractive for his peace of mind. Miss Lizzy Miller was the most alluring woman he'd met in his life. And she was also a woman he couldn't afford to allow himself to become attracted to. In his mind, the only woman he wanted to become involved with was one he could see himself marrying one day. Maybe it was his Amish upbringing, but he still thought that courting and walking out with a woman was the way to go. But that woman could not be Amish.

He was never going back, and he couldn't ask a fine woman such as Lizzy to leave the life she believed in. Which meant they had no future.

Get your mind back on the job, Isaac.

"I think the restaurant owner would be a wise one to watch." He responded to her earlier comment. "It's very possible that he might lead us to where Zave is hiding. I will ask the chief to have someone watch his place. And if we have reasonable suspicions, we might be able to get a search warrant."

"You can't get that now?"

"No, not without cause. All we have now is a man who doesn't want the police scaring away his customers. That's not a good enough reason to get a search warrant. Much as I wish it was."

Walking down the sidewalk toward his cruiser, Isaac spotted a skateboarder coming way too fast in their direction. The kid had his head down. All Isaac could see was the black helmet. It was unfortunate that this was a road with very little traffic. He grabbed Lizzy's hand and pulled her closer to him as the skater whizzed past them.

Electricity jolted from where their hands were connected and continued up his arm.

She jerked away, her face averted. He could see the flushed cheeks, though. She'd felt it, too. And judging by the distress in her wide blue eyes when she looked back up at him, she obviously didn't like it any more than he did.

They inched away from each other. When they arrived at the cruiser, Isaac stepped up to it and opened the passenger door for her.

The sound of an engine revving and tires screeching rent the air. Isaac's head snapped up, his eyes scanning for the source. Instinctively, he pressed Lizzy closer to the car to better shield her, his hand on her shoulder to silently tell her to stay down. She responded by ducking down slightly.

The Jeep responsible for the noise was coming toward them, moving too fast for safety. As it neared, a young man leaned out the passenger window of the Jeep roaring down the road towards them. Murderous rage glared from the young man's face.

It was Zave.

NINE

Zave leaned farther out the window. A gun glinted in his hand, aimed straight at Lizzy.

Isaac shoved the Amish woman to the ground and shielded her with his body. The cruiser provided extra cover for them. A shot rang out. It clanged as it struck the lamp pole at his left. Isaac heard the man swearing.

Snatching his own service revolver, he popped up to level a shot at the Jeep. His shot caught the back door of the vehicle as it swerved wildly around the corner.

"Come on!" Assisting Lizzy to her feet, he assessed her condition quickly. Assured that she was well, he gestured to the still-open door. "Get in. If we hurry, maybe we can catch up to him."

He ran around to his side of the cruiser and jumped in. As soon as they were in motion, he jabbed his radio to call in the shooting. He rattled off the license plate number, make and model of the vehicle. "Suspect was seen fleeing the scene and heading east on Randolph Avenue. Number four in pursuit. Request backup."

"Backup will be joining you en route. Number six has left the station."

Good. Ryder was on the way. Isaac steered his vehicle into a fast turn, feeling his wheels swerve out behind him. The tires squealed, but he managed not to hit the opposite curb.

Up ahead, he could make out the Jeep. It swung wide around another curve.

"Hold on!" he yelled across to Lizzy. He stomped his foot down on the gas and flipped on the lights and the siren. The car coming the other way slid to the side of the curb. Isaac flew past him.

"Come on. Come on." He clenched his hands on the steering wheel as his car inched closer and closer to the Jeep. He saw another cruiser behind him. It was Ryder. He wished Ryder had come in from the other direction in order to cut the Jeep off. However, it was too late for that.

The gates at the train tracks began to descend. It was like watching a bad movie. He watched, incredulous, as the Jeep wove in through the closing gates. Within seconds, he spotted an Amtrak train coming. To make matters worse, the train stopped to let passengers off and to allow others to board. By the time the gates rose again, the Jeep was nowhere in sight.

The two cruisers split up and continued to search, but the Jeep was gone.

"Hey, Ryder. I'm going back to the scene and see if any witnesses saw what had happened. Maybe someone will have more information than we have."

He doubted it. But he had to try.

Unfortunately, after an hour of walking the street a second time, they were no closer to finding any answers than they had been the first time. Unless you considered inciting an irate restaurant owner to declare that he would be coming in to complain about the police harassing him.

"May I ask you a question?" Lizzy snapped the buckle of her seat belt, then turned to watch him.

"Jah." He heard the word and grimaced. He didn't know why, but he'd just spoken in his Amish dialect. He had taken such pains to bury it to sound more *Englisch.* "What is it?"

"Why did you become a police officer? Why not a firefighter, or an ambulance driver?"

He heard what she really wanted to know. Why go into a career where it was necessary to carry a gun? Back when he was Amish, the only time he used a gun was for hunting. The Amish were pacifists. Extreme pacifists. He doubted his own *dat* would have picked up a gun to save his own life. To his *dat,* guns were for killing only.

"I had trouble picking up a gun when I first left my community," he mused, smiling slightly at the memory of how awkward he had been.

"Then why do it?"

He turned the corner. The road ahead was long and straight.

He considered her question. Did he really want to tell her the story? It wasn't like him to tell personal stories from his life to others. Even Ryder didn't know the whole story.

Maybe if she knew the story, it would break the connection growing between them.

Decision made, he thought for a second where to begin. It would only make sense if he went back to the very beginning.

"I grew up in a community only about fifteen miles from where your cousin lives," he told her. "I had two younger siblings. A sister named Mary and a younger brother named Joshua." Sorrow clogged his throat briefly as he let his mind dwell on his siblings. It had been so long since he had seen them. "Joshua was two years younger than I was. He also was blind. We'll never know the whole story, but when he was fifteen, some college kids out driving came upon him while he was standing near the road. We found out later that they were drunk. They had seen Joshua and stopped to ask him for directions. When they realized he was blind, the leader apparently decided that he would make a good target. They roughed him up a bit, taking the little of value that he had on him. When they left, he had staggered to his feet, and the car hit him. It never even slowed down. They left him in the street to die. My brother was taken to the hospital, but there was nothing they could do. He was in a coma for ten hours until he died the next morning."

Out of the corner of his eye, he saw her dab at her tears. Feeling bad for upsetting her, he started to apologize.

"Tell me the rest."

Surprised, he glanced at her. Her eyes were wet, but her sympathetic face was calm.

"Ironically, the boys were caught when the car they were driving was used to vandalize town property. Two of the boys turned on the group leader for lesser sentences. My father refused to attend the trial. He refused to see to it that the boys who killed his son were brought to justice. At the trial the two boys who were testifying against their friend swore before the court that he had hit Joshua on purpose, and that it hadn't been an accident as the other kid had said. His lawyer was smooth. By the time that he was done, it almost seemed that Joshua had been at fault for being out at night like that. What was he thinking would happen, a blind boy out near the street?

"The kid got a slap on the wrist, as the *Englisch* say. I was so angry. I blamed my father. Had he gone to the trial, I told him, maybe there would have been justice. Justice, he told me, belonged to God. I told him that maybe I no longer wanted to believe in the God that would let my brother die and let the one who killed him go free."

Lizzy gasped sharply, her hand flying to cover her mouth.

He nodded. "*Jah*, it was a horrible thing to say to him. He was shocked. And he looked older than he had ever looked before. He stared at me and told me that his son would never speak that way, and that until his son was ready to be respectful, the disrespectful young man standing in front of him was not welcome in his house."

He pulled into the police department parking lot. Disengaging the engine, he had one final thing to add. "So I left. I became a police officer to do my best to bring justice to those who are harmed by others, like my brother was. My father and I never spoke again. He died two years ago."

"I'm so sorry."

He shrugged. "We made our choices. I'm here now, and I have made a life for myself with good people. I am doing what I set out to do, and I don't plan to ever go back."

It was one of the saddest stories she had ever heard.

It also explained how an Amish man would become a police officer. Still, her heart broke. Not just for him. For his whole family. For his parents, who had lost both their sons. Had his father regretted his ultimatum? She thought about her own father. *Dat* had never made a promise that he hadn't meant. At least, not in her memory.

Lizzy followed Isaac into the police station, her mind still wrapped up in what he had told her. They had barely stepped inside when the chief approached them.

"Report, Isaac."

She watched as Isaac gave the chief his report. He was comfortable here. Not only that, but he was also clearly respected by his colleagues. He truly had made a life for himself.

What about faith? Where was God in his life?

She didn't know how she would have survived the trauma of being held captive if she hadn't had her faith. Even with her faith, she had come out scarred.

Such as her inability to trust men. But that wasn't completely true anymore. She trusted Isaac. And by association, she sort of trusted Ryder. Although she wasn't comfortable with him the way she was with Isaac.

The door opened. A woman entered the room, her eyes darting around nervously. Lizzy considered her intently, frowning. She felt she should know this woman, but from where? Her round cheeks and messy bun tickled an image in Lizzy's mind. She knew she'd seen her before but couldn't remember where.

Isaac saw the woman. His stance immediately straightened. "You were at the restaurant I visited today."

The woman blanched at being recognized but nodded her head. It was evident that the openness of the room made her uncomfortable. "I have information about the man you saw today. The owner was lying."

"Please, we can talk in the conference room." Isaac led the way. When she entered the room ahead of him, he gave Ryder a significant look.

"Lizzy, you stick with me," Ryder said.

Isaac joined them less than twenty minutes later. She knew by the way his eyes sparkled he had some good news. He pulled Ryder and Lizzy with him into the chief's office. Lizzy was not easy in the office, but she would have felt even less so out in the other room, so she kept silent.

The chief's gaze skittered over her briefly before settling on Isaac. He was grinning widely; a dimple flashed in his left cheek.

"It appears you have some news, Officer," the chief said, indicating he should spill it.

"Indeed, ma'am. That was a waitress from the restaurant we visited this afternoon. The restaurant where the owner had promised me, twice, that he had never seen Zave. Well, it seems he was lying through his teeth. That lady said that she overheard our conversation. She also happened to catch a glimpse of the picture I was showing him. No sooner had we left his restaurant than he went into the back office. Then a young man came out, grabbed a skateboard and helmet from the owner's nephew, and was on his phone calling someone to come pick him up."

Lizzy jumped to her feet. "He knew we'd been shot at and still told us he didn't know him! He even accused you of harassing him." She clenched her hands, fury seething and bubbling inside her at the gall of the man. She could have been killed, or Isaac could have been. Did the man not have a conscience?

"Hey, Lizzy. It's okay." Isaac came and stood in front of her. She stared at him in disbelief.

"Okay? How is something like this ever okay?"

His grin widened. "Remember me saying that we needed cause for a search warrant? Now we have one."

She bit her lip. That was what they wanted. But she still wasn't happy about how they got it.

She sighed. "Maybe *Gott* has decided to help us."

He gave her an odd look. "Maybe He has."

Her breath caught at the look in his eyes. All of a sudden, her senses were overwhelmed with his nearness. She could feel the static and sizzle between them. It was an impossible attraction. Stilling the part of her that wanted to draw closer to him, she stepped back and resumed her seat, aware that her cheeks were flushed.

If she wasn't careful, she would return home with a broken heart.

His grin dimmed. Maybe she was wrong, but it seemed that he was struggling with the same attraction.

He turned away from her, his expression more serious now. "Chief, how long do think it would take us to get a warrant?"

She tapped her chin. "It's almost four. Let me see if I can put a rush on it. I don't see us getting it before tomorrow, at the earliest."

He sighed. "That's what I thought."

"Isaac, you should be going off duty. Why don't you head out? We'll put Lizzy up in the new hotel on Water Street. Better security there, plus we'll have a guard on her door. No meals that don't come from us."

She wasn't taking any chances. Lizzy didn't want to go to any motel or hotel again. After what had happened before, she certainly didn't think she'd feel safe there, no matter how tight the security was, but what else could she do?

"That sounds like a plan." Isaac yawned abruptly. "Excuse me. Look, we're tired and hungry. I might drive her over there and we'll stop and pick up something to eat on the way. Go through a drive-through or something. At least that would solve the concern about room service."

Chief Carson waved them away. "Fine, fine. Go get something to eat. Plan to have her at the hotel in forty-five minutes. If you are going to be late, call it in so no one worries. Then go home and get some rest. I expect you to be back here tomorrow looking sharp."

"Yes, ma'am." Isaac clasped Lizzy's elbow in his hand briefly. She could feel the warmth of his hand long after he had removed it. She promised herself that she would stop letting his nearness disturb her. As they stepped outside, a breeze tickled her nose. She smelled the grass, still damp from the rain. And she smelled the french fries from the fast food restaurant two buildings down.

Another smell caught her attention. It was a clean aroma of shampoo and soap. A simple smell.

Isaac.

She put another six inches between them. Had he noticed? She sent him a glance under her lashes. He was watching her, a smile playing on his lips. Immediately, she looked away.

They got into the car and he drove them to the nearest drive-through. There really wasn't anything that appealed to her, so she settled on a chicken salad.

"Are you sure that will be enough for you?"

"*Jah.* I appreciate your concern. I'm not that hungry tonight."

"It's probably stress." He bit into a french fry. As he chewed, he twisted his lips. Obviously, the fries weren't to his liking. "I'm not that hungry, either. But we have to eat. Chief's orders, you know."

She laughed, but obediently dug into her salad. After a few moments, a scent she'd never smelled before caught her attention.

"What's that—"

"Smell." Isaac finished for her, his eyes wide. He pulled the vehicle over to the side of the road. He killed the engine and hit the door locks to open both sides. "Get out!"

She didn't even think about it. Lizzy shoved the door open and stumbled out of the car, her half-eaten salad tumbling to the ground. She ignored it. Isaac was at her side, grabbing her hand and pulling her with him away from the car.

They stopped. She saw the tightness of his eyes and followed his glance. And gasped.

Flames were shooting out from under his car.

He called 911. Within five minutes, he was assisting the other officers to clear the street. The fire truck arrived. By this time, Isaac's cruiser was fully engulfed in flames. The firefighters tried to get the fire out, but they gave up when it became clear that the blaze wouldn't be extinguished.

"I think it's an electrical fire!" she heard one of them holler.

"The fuel tank's going to blow!" another bellowed. "Take cover."

Isaac left his group and charged up the lawn to the park where she was standing. He grabbed her around the waist and half lifted her off her feet as he guided her deeper into the playground area. He pushed her under a slide, crowding in behind her. She felt his breath at the nape of her neck.

A huge roar filled the air. The air simmered with the heat of the blast. Debris fluttered around them. It was mostly ash.

Isaac made them wait another five minutes. When they emerged from under the slide, she stumbled at the sight of the destroyed cruiser. Black smoke curled from the flames still busily consuming what had been his car. Isaac placed his arm around her shoulders and hauled her up against his side to keep her steady. She didn't protest. He was the one calming presence in her world.

"Isaac!" Ryder ran up to them, his face drained of all color. "Are you guys all right? How did this even happen?"

Isaac glared at the wreckage, his face tight with anger.

"This was no accident. I can't prove it, but Zave was behind this. He needs to be taken down."

TEN

Despite her protests that she was uninjured, Lizzy was forced to once again undergo an examination by a paramedic. *Forced* might have been too strong a word. Isaac had been so concerned, she had given in to make him feel better.

The paramedic proclaimed her to be none the worse for wear.

"I told you I was fine," she murmured to the handsome officer who had not left her side since his car blew up. "You were worried for nothing."

"Not for nothing, Liz. You could have been seriously hurt, and I wasn't sure if you would tell me."

Her heartbeat bumped up its pace at the nickname. No one had ever called her Liz. It was always Elizabeth or Lizzy. One felt too old, and the other sometimes made her feel like she was still a child. But Liz was the name given to a woman. It might be a name she'd never be called by anyone else, but here, in this moment, she was Liz to a man who had saved her life at least twice.

It was a memory she'd treasure. A good one to keep alongside the bad.

"I would have told you, Isaac. If for no other reason than because you deserve the truth." She wouldn't look at him. His presence, so near her, was making it hard to keep her breathing even. Never had a man affected her this way. With most men, it was fear or anxiety. Isaac inspired none of that.

She knew it couldn't last. But would it really be wrong for her to enjoy it while it did?

Isaac stood. She glanced up from where she was sitting on the bumper of the ambulance and saw a new man approach. Richard, his shirt said. His hat bore the name of a mechanic shop.

"Rich," Isaac greeted him, shaking his hand. "Any news for me?"

"Yeah, but you're not going to like it, Yoder."

Lizzy raised her eyebrows. *Yoder?* It amused her.

Isaac saw her eyebrows and smiled back at her before returning his attention to the mechanic. "I'm sure I won't like it. Tell me, anyway."

"Your car had help catching on fire."

Isaac's face didn't change. "It was sabotaged."

"Sure was. Particularly, your electrical wiring was messed with. Wires cut and fused together. I'm guessing that whoever did this was hoping there wouldn't be enough evidence left to tell the car had been messed with." Richard wiped a forearm across his chin, leaving a streak of soot. Lizzy looked away to hide a smile. The only indication Isaac gave that he was amused was the slightest lift of one corner of his mouth. "Your guy's good," Richard continued. "The good news for you is that I'm better."

Isaac's grin erupted across his face. Lizzy smiled in response. "That you are, Rich. I appreciate the information."

They watched the mechanic saunter away. Silence fell between them, but it wasn't a heavy silence. Rather, it was comfortable. She realized that she had not felt this level of connection with anyone in such a long time.

The totaled cruiser was towed away, leaving scorch marks and ash in its wake. Lizzy shook her head. An hour ago, she had been sitting inside that car. What if they had been trapped inside it?

She shuddered.

Isaac slid his arm across her shoulders again. "Are you cold?"

She shook her head, wanting to snuggle closer into his warmth. "No. I was just thinking about that car. We came so close to being trapped inside it."

"You know what? All of this drama is making me rethink my thoughts about God."

She jerked away from him so she could stare into his face. "What do you mean? Rethink how?"

It would devastate her if he completely lost his faith due to her presence in his life.

He smiled at her, that beautiful half smile that made her breath catch and her pulse hammer through her veins.

"I don't mean anything wrong by it. Quite the opposite." He moved closer and held his hand down to her, silently offering her his assistance. She grasped his hand and allowed him to help her. When he squeezed her hand before letting it go, she had the absurd urge to lunge forward and grab his hand once more. She hid her hands in her cloak instead, chiding herself for being fanciful.

They began to walk. She wondered if he would continue.

"When I left my parents' house," he began again, "I was so angry. I was mad at *Dat*, but also at God. I hadn't lost my faith, but I also didn't trust Him to take care of me these past few years."

"So how has being in constant danger changed you?"

He laughed at her words. Her heart warmed at the sound, although she hadn't meant for her comment to be funny. She was absolutely serious.

"Here's the deal, Liz. There's been danger, but we've been cared for. We're still here, right?"

Hmm. She hadn't quite thought about it like that. Suddenly, she was ashamed at the lack of trust she had shown in her own life. She said she trusted God, but she hadn't trusted Him with her fears and her anxieties. In fact, the only one she'd trusted to help her manage her issues was herself.

That obviously hadn't been working out for her.

"What do we do now?" The sun was going down. She was more wary than ever about spending her night in a hotel room.

"I think I'm going to see if you can sleep somewhere at the station tonight," he announced.

She stopped. He walked a few more steps before he

noticed she'd not followed. When he glanced back, his brows were puckered. "What?"

"Sleep in the station? Isn't that kind of open? And there aren't many police officers there at night."

"It locks up. And I will be there, too. Not in the same room, obviously, but you'll have someone keeping watch. I need to check on something. Tomorrow, I'll have a new plan."

Sleeping in his desk chair outside of the conference room where Lizzy was sleeping on a rollaway cot was not going to be remembered as his most restful night ever. His shoulders, neck and back all ached. Standing, he stretched and winced as many of his muscles protested.

He'd fought over an idea all night. It had come to him in a moment of clarity as a solution to how he could protect Lizzy. The next moment he was relieved to discard it as far-fetched and unnecessary. After all, he reasoned, the visual artist should be able to come out in the next day or so. He had heard on the radio while he was brushing his teeth that the level of the floodwater was rapidly decreasing. Surely that meant she'd soon be there. With a picture of the perp to circulate, one with a clear image, they'd possibly be able to find their guy.

Lizzy joined him at six the next morning. He knew she hadn't slept well. There were dark circles under her blue eyes. She was past the point of being merely tired and was quickly rounding the corner to exhausted. He hated that she had to go through this. Still, he glanced up at her and she smiled as she came to join him. That smile was so genuine and so welcoming he immediately lost whatever he was thinking. That was a smile a man could watch his entire life with pleasure.

That jolted him.

He didn't have a lifetime to spend with her. He had a few more days, and then she'd be going back to her life and he'd still be here living his.

It would feel a whole lot emptier when she was gone.

Stop. He wasn't ready to deal with the ramifications of such thoughts or feelings, so he shoved them aside the best he could. And ignored the hollow sensation inside him. She was not meant to be his.

When he heard the chief enter the office, he nearly leaped to his feet with relief. Lizzy was eyeing him strangely, and he couldn't blame her. He was acting odd, but he was determined to keep himself distant from her. Which wasn't going to be easy, but he had to do it. She was a temptation he could not afford.

"Chief," he greeted his superior. "I heard on the radio this morning that the floodwater was going down. Think we could get the visual artist in here in the next day or so?"

The way she pressed her lips together and shook her head did not fill him with confidence. He had a bad feeling that he wasn't going to like what she said.

"Isaac," she said in a voice heavy with regret. "I am afraid that won't be possible. I talked with her boss this morning. He had called to let me know that she has taken some time off. It seems that she had a family emergency with her mother. She won't be back for a week."

A week. Seven days with Zave running around and leaving Lizzy with a target on her back. He shifted his gaze to the pretty blonde standing so close to him. She stuck out around here, especially riding around with the cops. You didn't often see women in full Amish attire sitting in a police cruiser.

The image of her lying on the floor after she'd been poisoned hit him like a semitruck. He couldn't let anyone hurt her again.

The idea he'd been trying to avoid came back to him. He forced himself to truly consider it. Sure, it would be uncomfortable for him. But it might be the only way to keep Lizzy safe. He had to try it. Even if he didn't like it.

The aroma of food preceded Ryder into the room. In his right hand, he carried two bags. A drink carrier with four tall coffees was in his left. Isaac's mouth watered as the salty smell of bacon, biscuits and hot coffee hit his nose. Next to him, Lizzy's stomach complained loudly. He laughed as she blushed and wrapped her arms around herself, as if to hold the rumbling and gurgling noises in.

"It's Ryder to the rescue!" Ryder strode over to them and deposited the bags carrying the food on the desk in front of him. "I have biscuits with bacon, eggs and cheese here, and coffee—" he set the drink carrier down with a flourish "—here. Help yourselves. For you, Chief." He pulled a bottled water from his pocket and handed it to Chief Carson. She didn't smile, but her dark eyes were definitely sparkling.

"Why, thank you, Ryder. I guess if you ever get tired

of being an officer, you could become a waiter at some fancy establishment."

"If she just insulted me, I don't want to know," he said to Isaac.

Isaac chuckled. He picked up a wrapped sandwich and gave it to Lizzy. She was already opening a coffee. As she peeled back the tab, she held it under her nose and sniffed in appreciation. She accepted the sandwich. *"Denke."*

While they ate, Isaac brought Ryder up to speed. His buddy looked at Lizzy with a speculative air. "Lizzy, no offense, but if you stay here another week, it might be hard to hide you. You do sort of stand out, you know, dressed like you are."

She set her sandwich down, her eyes growing wide, apprehension deep in their depths. Her brow furrowed as she began to gnaw on her lower lip.

Isaac glared at Ryder, despite the fact that he had been thinking the same thing less than thirty minutes before. He didn't like the fact that Ryder was upsetting his girl.

Wait. One. Minute. He did not just think that. Lizzy was a wonderful young woman, and they had seemed to click, but she was not his girl. Nor was there a possibility that they would ever be together on a permanent basis. He needed to remember that.

Even if he wished she were.

"What are you glaring at me for?" Ryder demanded. "Don't you think she's fairly conspicuous? Maybe we should consider having her wear ordinary *Englisch* clothes for the time being."

Now she was looking really alarmed. Isaac understood. For her to wear *Englisch* clothes, even to blend in, would be going against the rules of her church. If her bishop found out, she could be in serious trouble. One did not conform to save their life.

"Don't ask that of her." He spoke up before Ryder could continue. "Her manner of dress is part of her entire belief system. It defines her. And you don't ask an Amish woman to allow any man who isn't her husband see her hair."

He could feel the eyes of everyone in the room on him. When he glanced at the only one whose opinion he actually thought mattered in this situation, he was relieved to note the gratitude in Lizzy's expression. He had been right to speak up.

"What options do we have, Isaac?" Chief Carson sat on the edge of a desk facing them. There was no criticism in her voice, nor did he see any on her face. Instead, she appeared truly interested in his opinion on the matter.

He breathed in deep, preparing himself to say words that he had never expected to say. "I think I should take her to stay with the Amish community I grew up in. She could stay with my family."

Ryder's jaw fell open, part of his biscuit still unchewed.

Lizzy swung around to face him, her face going still.

Only Chief Carson appeared unaffected by his statement.

"How would that help? This Zave knows he's looking for an Amish woman."

Isaac began to pace, talking out loud as he tried to hash out his thoughts into some semblance of an intelligent idea. "She's Amish, yes, but not from here. If Zave knew Bill Allister, which we can assume he did, then he probably also knows that Bill was from LaMar Pond, Pennsylvania, and not from southwestern Ohio. Why would he search for her there? He's seen her with me, but I have never been dressed in Amish clothing, so he has no way of connecting me to the Amish communities nearby. She would completely blend in there, giving her time and space while we wait for either our visual artist to return or another one to be brought in."

"Sound thinking, except for one thing," Chief stated. "The Amish are peaceful people. There would be no way to protect her there."

This was where he really needed extra air. He knew what he should say, but the words wanted to stick in his throat. He cleared it, twice. "Yes, there would. Because I would go with her."

ELEVEN

Lizzy was stunned at Isaac's suggestion. For a moment, she was unable to speak. Then the words broke free and rushed out of her. She could not allow Isaac to make this sacrifice for her. What about his family? Wouldn't she bring danger to his family?

"*Nee*, Isaac! You cannot do this! It's not a *gut* plan."

It was his turn to be speechless. He stopped pacing and stared at her. After a second or two, his eyebrows rose in question. "How is this not a *gut* plan, Liz?"

His sensible voice, and the use of his personal nickname for her, only made her more stubborn. "You know why. What if your mother is angry at you and won't let you stay? And even if she does let us stay with her, you said I could not go to my family because that would bring danger to them. How is this any different?"

"She's got a point, Isaac," Ryder opined from the side.

"*Jah*, she does." Isaac crossed his arms across his chest, still managing to look handsome even while he was being obstinate. He probably didn't even realize how Plain he was sounding at the moment. "Lizzy, your family would have been in danger because of the possibility that Zave could link them to you. The Allister family had been driving yours for years. You said so yourself."

"So?"

She wasn't going to like this. He was going to use logic. "So—" he drew the word out "—we already know that Sue's place was tossed and that she is missing. It's possible that Zave wanted information about you, the Amish girl that Bill was driving. We know that he is aware you saw him. Would Sue have known where you were headed?"

She paled. "Sue's driven me to my cousin's house before. And to my aunt and uncle's—Addie's parents'—house. My family is in danger!" she gasped. Had Zave gone to her family?

He was shaking his head. "I already thought of that. Your uncle is aware of the danger. He has agreed to contact the police in the area if anything suspicious happens, or if there is any trouble."

She needed to sit down, she thought as the sudden panic drained out of her, leaving her legs feeling weak. She collapsed into a chair. Isaac left his position near the wall and strode over to her, crouching so they were almost eye to eye.

"There is no reason why Zave should think to look at my family. The two communities aren't connected in any way. And if my mom won't let me stay, I'm sure we can think of something else. I wasn't shunned or actually kicked out of the community, so there's a good chance we would succeed. I really think we should give it a try."

She tilted her head to the side to study him. A bit more of the ice she'd built around her heart melted away.

"You're going to be the one to stand out," she murmured, some of the argument leaving her. "Not many policemen live in Amish communities."

He smiled, but she heard his swallow. "I'll be undercover."

"Undercover?"

He sighed. "I'll be dressed as an Amish man. So I will blend in."

"Will your bishop allow that?" Chief Carson asked from behind him. Isaac stood, his ears a bit pink.

Lizzy had forgotten that others were present, and it seemed he had, as well.

"I'll have to check on that. Of course, we'll have to respect his wishes if he says no. But it's worth a shot."

"Agreed." She nodded decisively. "I will send someone over there to ask. I want you two to lie low for the moment until we find out one way or another whether we can pull this crazy idea of yours off."

"Um, Chief?"

"Yes, Isaac?"

"If we are able to do this, I can't be seen driving to the community. Plus, it would be a dead giveaway if my truck was spotted at my old house."

A chuckle off to the side had her gaze swinging over to where Ryder was lounging against a desk, his legs straight out in front of him. "That would defeat the purpose, wouldn't it?"

They all laughed along with the sarcastic officer, but Lizzy couldn't dispel the sense of guilt that had started to blossom inside her. Part of her was hoping that going to his home would encourage Isaac to return to his family and to the Amish way of life. It was a selfish wish, though, based on her wish that they could allow the attraction between them to develop along the natural course it might take if they were two young Amish people courting. Her cheeks flushed.

If Isaac ever returned to the Amish life, it couldn't be because of her. That would be shortsighted. And what happened if he grew tired of that life and wanted to return to the *Englisch* world? He was an honorable man, so he probably wouldn't desert her.

No, he'd just stay and start to resent her for being the reason he was stuck in a life he didn't want.

Her heart grew so heavy. She could not bear the thought of being the person to hold him back.

"Lizzy? You okay? Looking pretty somber there."

Startled out of her reverie, she lifted her head to find that they were alone in the office. Where had everyone gone?

"I'm sorry. I wasn't paying attention. I didn't notice the chief and Ryder leaving."

He shrugged. "No problem. The chief is going to see about getting the bishop's permission. A friend of hers is the sheriff near my old community and she's going to ask him to visit the bishop. Ryder will try to hurry the search warrant for the restaurant. We'll wait here and stay safely out of sight. If we do go to my house, I want my face out in public as little as possible, although

Zave has obviously already seen me. Enough that he recognized which number was on my cruiser."

His lips twisted. She sighed. "I'm sorry that your car was destroyed."

"Yeah, me, too. But it could have been worse. And no one was hurt, so that's good."

She nodded, noticing for the first time how quiet the office was. With no one else around, it seemed uncomfortably intimate. She bit her lip. It wasn't approved of for a young woman of courting age to be alone with a single young man. True, there were extenuating circumstances, but she knew her father wouldn't approve.

Knowing that they were both stranded in the empty office for the time being, she frantically searched for a topic of conversation. Anything to detract from the tension she could feel sizzling between them. She flicked a sidelong glance at him through her lashes. He was looking directly at her, his blue-gray eyes deep and intense. The tension thickened. Her heart fluttered, even as her stomach flipped. When she realized she was breathless, she turned her head away from him, trying to regain her equilibrium.

She was twenty years old, not a young girl!

Another thought struck her. Whatever else she might have been feeling, she was not feeling anxiety. Excitement and anticipation, but not anxiety. The novelty of it calmed her, as she reflected with some awe on this turn of events.

Isaac sat down across from her. Their knees almost touched, but not quite. The urge to close the distance was disturbing. She needed to break the silence.

"What was the hardest thing to get used to when you left your community?" Maybe it wasn't the most polite question to ask, but she owned to being very curious. "My sister was always amazed by how much people talked. Even though she was deaf and couldn't hear it, it seemed like people were always either texting or calling each other, or just talking."

He rubbed his chin. She was relieved to see that he didn't appear to be insulted. "Let me think. I was amazed at how everyone seemed to be in a hurry. It didn't matter what they were doing. Driving, writing, talking. Even eating. There was always somewhere they had to be, and people were always talking about being late."

She nodded. "*Jah.* I have seen that, too."

From there, they talked about several different subjects, and slowly the tension eased off. Before she knew it, they were laughing together over stories of trouble they'd gotten into as children.

"I can't believe that you got into so much mischief!" Isaac exclaimed, grinning.

"*Jah,* I was not a well-behaved child. I was always too curious! And my mother despaired because I would never walk. Always, I would run. Not because I was in a hurry. I just liked the feeling of moving fast. Especially with bare feet. Ack! I hated wearing shoes. My *mamm* tells me that for the first five years of my life, I was always walking around barefoot. Even when they managed to get shoes on me, I would take one off. Always the left foot. It didn't matter where I was. It wasn't uncommon for me to walk around with only one shoe.

According to my family, there are still left-side shoes out there somewhere that they've never found."

They laughed. She hugged her arms around her waist when her sides started to ache.

He stopped laughing suddenly. She chuckled and looked over at him.

And suddenly her laughter got stuck in her throat.

The expression on his face was unmistakable. She couldn't breathe. He wanted to kiss her.

And she wanted to let him.

It would be so easy to lean forward and kiss those pink lips. He wanted to kiss her more than he wanted his next breath. When he glanced into her eyes, he was lost. She wanted him to kiss her as much as he did.

Without thinking about it, he started to lean forward. He was so close he could feel her breath on his face. He leaned in, just a little closer. Her eyes drifted shut.

Just before their lips could touch, a door slammed open, jolting him to his senses. Ryder's voice came clearly from the hall. Isaac leaped to his feet and all but ran to the other side of the room, where he paced while he willed his wild pulse to cease hammering in his veins. His face was hot. He raked his hands through his hair.

What had he been thinking? He had almost kissed her, here in his office. He cast an agonized glance over at Lizzy. Her cheeks were red, and he could see that her hands were tightly clasped in her lap. She was biting her lip.

Was she mad at him? Offended? He had no idea what

was going through her mind. They weren't walking out together or courting. They weren't even in a position to ever be doing either of those.

"I'm sorry," he whispered, his voice hoarse in the quiet room. "I never meant for that to happen."

She nodded but didn't respond.

"Lizzy, did I offend you?"

Finally, her head lifted and she speared him with a glistening glance. Man, he'd made her cry. He had been feeling bad. Now he felt horrible.

"I'm not mad at you, Isaac. I'm upset at myself."

He blinked. "Mad at yourself? What for? You didn't do anything wrong."

She gave a bitter laugh. "Isaac, I am not a child. I am twenty years old. I know better than to be in situations like this where such things happen. I also know better than to kiss a man who is not part of my culture. *Nee*, this is not your fault. At least, not completely. I could have pulled back. I made the choice not to, and that was selfish of me."

He felt hollow inside. When she stated the facts as she saw them so clearly, he saw that, in her mind, he was not an acceptable choice for her. He had already known this and had admitted it to himself, but to hear the words spoken out loud by the woman he had nearly kissed, well, it just made his spirits sink.

"Hey, guys! Guess what I found out?" Ryder sauntered into the room, completely oblivious to the vibes bouncing between Isaac and Lizzy. Isaac was good with the distraction.

"What?"

"Sid and his mother and sister have been moved to witness protection. Sid has agreed to testify if Zave can be brought to court. The kid has courage, I'll say that for him."

"I am so happy that he and his family are safe!" Lizzy exclaimed. She moved to stand near the men, keeping several feet between herself and Isaac. While he understood why, it still bothered him.

Ryder started to head out of the office. "Oh." He turned back to them. "The chief said for me to tell you that you're all clear on Operation Amish. I'm to drive you there this evening. She figured that it might be easier if you went after dark. That way, you'd be less visible in the car, you know?"

"We'll be ready," Isaac responded. His stomach, though, was flipping like he'd swallowed a bullfrog. Ryder tossed another grin their way and then left the room.

He was going to see his family, after seven long years. How would they react? Would his sister, Mary, even recognize him? Would he recognize her? She'd been ten when he left, so she was just about seventeen now. The same age he had been when he left. And his *mamm*. Did she look much older? His insides quivered. Did she blame him for what had happened? She was letting him back into her home, surely that meant something.

A hand touched his. Lizzy slid her hand under his and turned it so that they were clasping fingers. It wasn't a romantic hold. He could see it in her eyes. She was offering her understanding and her support. He squeezed her fingers, letting her know he appreciated the gesture.

"It will be all right, Isaac. I know it's not easy, but trust *Gott*. He will help you through this. And I'll do whatever I can to make this easier for you."

"You are amazing, you know that?" he said. Her eyes widened in surprise. "No, I'm serious. Someone is after you, you are being told you can't go home, and yet here you are, offering me comfort. Thank you."

Two hours later, he was grateful for her supportive presence as Ryder's truck motored toward his mother's house. He could feel every bump and dip in the road. He was sure that Lizzy, who was sitting in the middle, could, too. She kept reaching out and bracing herself on the dashboard.

Ryder muttered apologies every time they encountered a particularly harsh bump, but other than that, the ride progressed smoothly. There was very little conversation. Ryder told them stories, but both Isaac and Lizzy were too tense to do more than offer token responses.

It was a little after seven in the evening when Isaac directed his friend to turn up his family's driveway. Ryder nodded and spun the wheel. The sounds of the truck suddenly sounded loud. "You should probably get the muffler checked out," Isaac muttered. It sounded so much louder out here than in the busyness of the town.

"Yeah. Maybe." Ryder shifted into Park in front of the house.

Isaac drew in a deep breath, then shoved open the door. He slid out of the truck, then offered Lizzy a hand to assist her out of the vehicle. Ryder left the motor running as he exited. Clearly, he wasn't intending on sticking around once he knew that his friend was indeed welcome at his childhood home.

The front door creaked open. A young woman of seventeen stepped out. She was lovely in the faded light. Isaac couldn't see every detail clearly, but he knew her eyes would be brown, and her hair would be a light brown. The dress she was wearing was dark. Blue, or maybe purple, he guessed.

"Mary," he greeted her, his voice taking on a definite rasp.

"Isaac." Her voice was shy, but not unwelcoming. It was too much to ask her to give him a hug, he supposed.

No sooner had the thought entered his mind than his little sister was launching herself off the porch and into his arms. His throat squeezed shut.

She released him and turned to Lizzy.

"This is my friend, Lizzy."

To his surprise, she embraced Lizzy. "Thank you! It's because of you that my brother is home again."

"Um." Lizzy glanced his way warily. "You're welcome. But—"

Mary waved the protests away. "I know. He's here for a short time. We also know about the man who is chasing you. *Gott* will take care of you, though. He always does."

Isaac opened his mouth to respond to his sister, but he never uttered the words. An older woman stepped out onto the porch. Her hands were covering her mouth, and even in the gathering darkness, he could see the glisten of her eyes as she fought against the tears.

She reached for him and he surged forward, taking her in his arms. "Hello, *Mamm*."

TWELVE

Lizzy's eyes grew hot as she watched the reunion between mother and son. Ryder pulled her aside for a moment and said his goodbyes.

"Do you still have that phone that Isaac gave you?"

She started. "I had forgotten about it, but yes, I still have it."

He nodded. "Good. Use it if you need to."

Isaac separated from his family long enough to wish his friend a safe journey back to Waylan Grove. As the truck roared down the drive and out onto the street, Lizzy shivered. Her shoulder blades twitched. Standing out in the open like this, she felt like they were all vulnerable.

"Lizzy?" Isaac's warm breath tickled her ear. She shivered again.

"I feel like we're not safe standing out here."

His hand briefly gripped her shoulder, letting her know that he was there for her. She could grow very used to such things, she mused before turning her back on the thought.

"*Mamm*, Mary, let's go inside, yes?" Isaac's mother nodded and ushered her guests into her home.

Lizzy crossed the threshold and felt the comfort of being in a familiar setting. She had never been in this home before, but she had spent her life in Plain homes. The simplicity and the well-cared-for interior called to her, comforted her.

Isaac's mom, whose name she discovered was Ruth, was thrilled to have her son back in her home. Lizzy didn't want to be in the way during this reunion, so she asked to be shown to her room, with the intention of resting.

"I'll show you," Mary volunteered.

To her surprise, Isaac followed her to the bottom of the stairs. "Where's the phone I gave you?"

"Ryder asked me the same thing," she remarked, drawing the phone out of her apron.

He nodded. "I know we're here for our safety and that our plan is to blend in. However, I think we still need to be smart. I'm putting my number in this phone. If you need to call me in an emergency, I'm number two on the speed dial." He quickly modeled using the speed dial feature on the phone. "Hopefully, you'll never need to use it. But I would rather you knew how and not need it than be left helpless and in danger."

She took the phone from him when he was through. Their fingers brushed against each other, sending sparks and shivers up her arm. The intense longing that came with it had her pulling back. Did she imagine the regret on his face?

"Good night, Isaac."

Before she could change her mind, she ran lightly up the stairs to where Mary was waiting for her. She liked Isaac's sister. The girl was quiet, but she had a certain wryness in her voice. Lizzy wouldn't have been shocked if she discovered that under her shy and demure demeanor, Mary had a mischievous streak.

In her room, she prepared for bed.

Before she got under the covers, she walked to the window and knelt by the windowsill. There were no curtains. She had gotten used to having them, as the bishop in her district allowed them in bedroom windows for modesty's sake. She knew that in many districts, curtains were not allowed.

It was very easy to imagine someone peering up at her window in the darkness.

Where was Zave? Had he started to search for her?

And Sue, poor Sue! She prayed that her friend was still alive. What had they wanted from her? Was her home really destroyed in an effort to locate Lizzy? Isaac had thought it was a possibility. She hated the thought that someone would hurt her friend just to find Lizzy.

What kind of person would do such a thing?

Outside, a steady rain began to fall against the house. The drops splashed against the window, smearing the view. Leaving her spot, she went to the bed and lay down, pulling the comforter snug against her chin.

She was warm, and the bed had just the right amount of firmness. The house she was in was comfortable, and the people were welcoming. She'd had a very long day, and she was so tired she could feel it all the way down to her bones.

But tired as she was, she didn't think she'd be able to sleep well, knowing that Zave was still out there, searching for her.

Her God was bigger, though. He would see her through this. Hadn't He given her a strong protector in Isaac, one who she knew would step in front of a bullet for her? She always insisted that she had faith in God, yet she refused to hand over control of her life and how she would live it, a decision based on fear, not on truth and light.

"The Lord is my light and my salvation; whom shall I fear? The Lord is the strength of my life; of whom shall I be afraid?" She whispered into the dark, the words of Psalm 27:1 coming to her mind.

Determined to trust God in the days and trials to come, she resolutely shut her eyes.

"I am so happy to see you home, my son. Tell me about this danger your friend is in."

Isaac gazed into his mother's face, the flickers of the candles she had lit casting shadows across the familiar planes. She looked a little older, but her voice, her laugh and her smile were the same. Could she really have forgiven him? He kept waiting for the words of recrimination, or for the taint of bitterness in her tone. But he never heard it. As amazing as it might seem, it appeared that she had completely forgiven him for his role in tearing the family apart. He was humbled by the grace she extended to him.

At the very least, he had expected some comment

about how he had disappointed his father. About how his father had died waiting for him to come back.

Even that never came.

"I can't tell you everything that happened. What I can tell you is that Lizzy witnessed someone getting shot. And now she is being hunted, most likely because she is the one person who can identify the shooter. We have reason to believe that the man knows where she lives. We thought her coming here would be the safest place for her."

"It will be well. *Gott* has a plan for this."

How could she be so calm about it all? Even as he wondered it, he wished for just a small measure of the faith that had carried his mother through so much. Had he ever had this much faith? Maybe if he had, things would've been different when Joshua died.

Had he been wrong to go against his father?

No, he couldn't let himself get distracted by these questions. Not now. He was in the middle of something far too intense to allow his attention to wander. There was something he wanted to know, though.

"Do you think…" He paused, pondering the question he was about to ask his mother. Not sure if he really wanted to know the answer.

"What, Isaac? Please, tell me what's in your heart?" His mother leaned forward, letting him see the love and concern on her face.

He braced himself. "Do you think *Dat* ever forgave me before he died? We said some pretty unkind things to each other."

She sighed. "Your *dat*, he was a *gut* man. When

Joshua was killed, it tore him apart. I know you didn't see that. You were in so much pain yourself. Your *dat* clung to his faith, knowing that *Gott* is all-knowing and that He would see that justice was done."

He nodded. He knew all this.

"When you questioned our way of life, it hurt him, too." Isaac hung his head. His mother touched his arm. "Isaac, after his anger cooled, he realized that he had allowed his own fear to get in the way. He forgave you, and I know he prayed that you would forgive him and return."

He was stricken. "*Mamm*, I didn't know that."

"He let *Gott* have the anxiety. He died content, knowing that you were in *Gott*'s hands. He believed that one day He would bring you home. And here you are."

He needed to correct that misconception. "I'm not home for good, *Mamm*. I am here because my friend is in need. I have promised to protect her and to help her find the man who is trying to kill her. Once that's done and the man is behind bars, I will go back to my life as a cop."

"And Lizzy?"

Oh, no. He knew that tone. Somehow in just a few short moments, his mother had understood that the blonde woman sleeping upstairs had wormed her way into her wayward son's heart. He had to shut this down, now.

"*Mamm*, she's my friend. That's it."

She smiled. "I know that."

"Seriously, there's nothing more going on between us. And even if there was, it wouldn't last. She's baptized in the church. I would never ask her to leave. And I don't think that I can ever return."

"It will be as *Gott* intends," was all she would say.

Later, he was in his old room next to the kitchen. He had told his mother that he didn't think he could ever return. That bothered him. He hadn't said that he would never return. It was a small difference, but he knew himself well enough to know that he was starting to question his past decisions. And he was questioning what he wanted in his life.

It didn't matter. Even if he did want to return, and even if he was interested in pursuing a future with Lizzy, it could never happen. He had promised his brother that he would work for justice for those who were downtrodden. That still remained. So even if it made him unhappy, he was bound by that promise to continue.

The duty that had given his life purpose was beginning to feel like a stone around his neck.

THIRTEEN

Slipping back into his former way of life wasn't as difficult as Isaac had thought it would be. He woke up the next morning and dressed in the clothes his mother had found for him. He'd grown a bit since he was seventeen, both in height and in muscle. For a few minutes, he stood in the center of his room, dressed in the blue trousers and the suspenders, and dealt with the sense of déjà vu. It felt odd not to have his weapons belt on.

The quietness of the farm was a shock to his senses. He had gotten used to the music pounding from his neighbor's apartment. The slamming doors above him, the traffic outside his window. Here, he literally woke up with the rooster crowing. He shrugged off the disorientation and made his way to the kitchen, where he grabbed a cup of coffee before he headed out to the barn. He could hardly stay at his mother's house and not pitch in with the chores.

It wasn't long before the familiar rhythm of the chores came back to him. It took him longer than it used to, but he knew that within a few days it would feel as though he'd never left.

He wasn't here to do farm chores all day, though. As soon as the sun was up in the sky, he left the shelter of the barn and began to walk the perimeter. He stopped several times along the way, hearing movement. Most of the time, he was able to find the source of the noise. Twice, however, he wasn't.

He didn't like that. Not at all. While he doubted that they would have been found, especially this quickly, he wasn't about to take any chance.

Returning to the house, he went to his bedroom and sent Ryder and the chief a quick text. Then he returned to the kitchen. His mother and Lizzy were both up, and the tantalizing smell of breakfast wafted to him, making him realize how long ago it was since he ate.

The women were speaking in the dialect of German he had grown up with as he entered. He stopped and listened for a few minutes. He hadn't spoken that dialect, really spoken it, other than a few isolated words, in seven years. There were a few words he had forgotten, but he was able to catch the drift of the conversation.

"Good morning, *Mamm*. Lizzy."

Both women turned to smile at him. His heart lurched at the loveliness of the two women he loved most side by side.

He stumbled a moment, caught off his stride by the thought. He did not love Lizzy, he denied to himself. He admired her. He liked her very much. But he most definitely did not love her.

You keep telling yourself that.

The very idea terrified him more than facing an armed criminal. Because there was absolutely nothing he could do about it if he did love her. And once she was gone, he'd be left with a hole in his heart in the shape of Lizzy Miller.

"Good morning, Isaac," Lizzy greeted him. The full smile she'd first worn when she had seen him had shrunk to a small, hesitant smile. Possibly because he had stood there so long in a daze over his own thoughts.

He needed to get himself under control, right now.

"Listen, I was outside checking on things. I'm probably overreacting, but I sent a text to my boss and asked for my friend Ryder to drop off one of the dogs I've trained."

"A dog?" His mother frowned.

"She's not a pet," he told her. "She's been trained to aid in investigations. She would be a valuable help to ensure Lizzy's safety."

Lizzy grinned. "Is he bringing Lily?"

He smiled at her enthusiasm. "If the chief agrees, then that's the plan. But until she arrives, I need to ask you to stay in the house."

Her smile disappeared and was replaced by a scowl. She had obviously thought she'd have a bit more freedom once they were back in Amish country. He would love to allow her to have her way, but her safety came first. He couldn't be swayed by her wishes. Not in something this important.

"*Jah*, you should listen to my son, Lizzy. He's right. We want to return you safely to your family."

Did she look as stricken by the idea as he felt? But it was good that his mother had reminded them that she would be going home soon. It hadn't been an accidental warning on his mother's part. He remembered last night's conversation. His mother had guessed his feelings were growing for Lizzy. And she'd be happy to see them get together—if Isaac returned to the Amish church. She would never condone him wooing Lizzy away to the *Englisch* world. Son or not, she would do what she could to keep that from happening.

The conversation changed when Mary skipped into the room. He saw the wariness in Lizzy's eyes, though she smiled and tried to act as if she wasn't disturbed. When breakfast was finished, though, she sidled close to him.

"Do you think Zave has found us?" she whispered, her eyes darting to his face.

He lifted his coffee mug to his lips, taking a sip as he gauged whether either his *mamm* or Mary was listening in. When he was sure they weren't, he answered in a soft voice. "I hope not. It seems unlikely that he would have found us this quickly. But I'm not willing to take any chances with your safety on the line."

She frowned. The lost look on her face tugged at his heart. He wanted to sling his arm around her shoulders and pull her close to him, but he refrained. He did allow himself to shift two inches closer to her. She didn't appear to notice.

"It's scary how quickly I let my guard down," she mused. "Last night, I went to bed and I didn't think I'd sleep. But I did. And waking up to the familiar sounds of the farm, I somehow convinced myself that I was safe here. It's not true, though, is it? Until Zave is caught, I'll never be safe."

"Liz." He waited until her eyes lifted. He held her gaze. "I will do everything humanly possible to protect you. I promise you that I will." He hesitated. Did he dare? "I also have been thinking that we have God on our side. He has kept us from injury so far. I know that you know this, but I'm trying to trust Him to protect us, too."

She didn't say anything. She didn't need to. He could tell by the way her eyes glistened that his words had struck a chord with her. She lifted a hand to his face and placed it softly on his cheek. Butterfly soft and only for a moment, she allowed her hand to remain. Then it was gone and she was moving away from him.

He might have imagined it, but he could still feel her hand on his cheek.

Ryder arrived with Lily around nine. The German shepherd trembled with joy as she jumped out of the truck. She wasn't working, so he allowed himself to give her a two-handed rub along her back. She licked his face.

"Hey, I missed you, too, girl." He said it softly, but Ryder still heard him and snickered.

Isaac straightened. "You up to running the perimeter with us?"

Ryder patted his service weapon on his hip. "Always."

Giving the dog the command that she was on duty, Isaac led her around to seek out any danger lurking. Lily was young, but she took her duties seriously. He felt better knowing that she would be there, helping him to watch over Lizzy.

* * *

The next two days passed without incident. There had been no further sightings of Zave, and Isaac finally told her she could leave the house. As long as she had Lily with her. Lily had been given the command to guard Lizzy. Consequently, whenever she walked outside the house, she had either her canine shadow or Isaac with her.

She didn't leave the property, though. Isaac was still unsure of the safety outside of his family's home. She was fine with that. As much as she itched to have some sense of freedom back, she knew that she could not do anything to risk the family or to announce her presence in the area.

That didn't stop people from dropping by to visit them. Word had gotten around that Ruth's son had returned and had brought a young woman with him. A young Amish woman. Most of the people were hoping to hear that he had returned to the church and wondered if Lizzy and he were courting. Of course, most never asked. They hinted, but very few were bold enough to suggest such a thing. Lizzy gritted her teeth at all the attention but said very little. It was hard to remain inconspicuous when everyone within three miles was coming by to catch a glimpse of her. She felt like she was living under a magnifying glass.

"Ruth?" she asked on the third morning, walking outside to where the older woman was hanging a load of laundry on the line. Lizzy grabbed a shirt and pinned it up. "I haven't seen Isaac this morning. Not since breakfast."

Ruth secured a dress to the line and nodded. "*Jah.*

He decided to do a quick walk around to see if anyone has seen or heard anything strange. He said that we should stay close to the house. He should be back soon. He left Lily with us."

Of course he did. She looked at the dog and had the distinct impression of a soldier on guard. She wished he had said something to her before he left, but shrugged the feeling off. Isaac did not need to report his every move to her. She knew that whatever he was about, her safety was at the root of it.

Isaac still hadn't arrived half an hour later when one of the teenage daughters of Ruth's friend from a few blocks away drove up, her buggy clattering as she parked it in front of the house. The desperate look on the girl's face made Lizzy pay attention.

"Annie, what is it?" Ruth came out to see what was happening.

"It's *Mamm*!" the girl panted. "Something's wrong."

Ruth's face lost some of its color. "Is it the baby?"

"*Jah.* We have sent for the doctor, but the clinic is an hour away." The girl tried to hold herself together, but the tears fell down her cheeks, anyway.

Lizzy made a snap decision. "Ruth, I will go with her." When Ruth started to protest, she put her hand on the older woman's shoulder. "I'm a midwife. This is what I do."

She saw relief flood the girl's face at her words. She could not put her safety above the life of this woman and her baby. "I will take Lily with me. As soon as Isaac gets back, tell him where I am. He can meet me there."

She climbed up on Annie's buggy, making room for

Lily, who hopped up next to her. Annie scrambled up on the other side and took the reins.

"Tell me what is happening with your mother."

The girl gave a jerky description. By the time she came to an end, they were parked in front of another house. Lizzy understood the fear. The poor woman wasn't due to have her baby for six weeks. Although Lizzy strongly suspected that the woman may be having twins from the description of how quickly she had gained weight, as well as how carefully she was being monitored. It didn't surprise her that the daughter wouldn't know. Many families didn't even talk about the baby on the way with the other children until it was born. Lily went inside and found a woman who might have been in her early thirties, obviously in labor. Judging from the size of her belly, twins were a definite possibility. Lizzy put her training to use. By the time the doctor from the clinic arrived, one of the twins had been born and his sibling would be on the way shortly. She stayed until the second boy had been delivered.

Isaac hadn't arrived yet. She had expected him to be outside waiting for her.

Uncomfortable in the strange house, and not wanting to be in the way, she went outside and waited for another five minutes.

"What do you think, Lily?" she asked the dog. Lily's ears perked up at her name. "Should we start walking? Isaac is probably on his way. We'll probably meet up with him."

He would not be pleased that they had left. She should stay. But she didn't like the way the doctor had watched her. He didn't appear to be mean, only suspicious of her. No, she didn't want to stay here. With Lily by her side, she should be safe. And it was only a few blocks away. It had taken five minutes to drive there. She could be back at Ruth's in half an hour. It had been a fairly straight route, too, so she wasn't concerned about losing her way.

Her decision made, she headed out, the dog at her side. She did try to stay off the road as much as possible. The one side of the road was bordered by a thick, dense wood, so she figured if she saw anyone or heard anything, she would run in there and hide.

They had traveled about half the distance when the space between her shoulder blades began to tingle. She twitched her shoulders. Looking around, she tried to see who was watching her, but didn't see anyone. There was a scraping sound off to the left.

Lily growled. The sound stopped. That's when she realized that what she had been hearing was footsteps.

The hairs on the nape of her neck stood on end. She was being followed.

Urging the dog forward, she quickened her pace. The scraping started again. Was the person dragging their feet?

Gasping, she broke into a run, Lily keeping pace at her side.

She heard her name being called. Isaac! He was standing beside a buggy, but the horse was not attached to it. She ran up to him and threw her arms around him. He hugged her tightly, then set her back and searched her face.

"Are you hurt? Why were you running?"

She remembered the sound. "I think we were being followed." She looked around. "Why is your horse off the buggy?"

He pointed to the wheel. "It broke. I didn't want to risk injuring the horse while I tried to fix it."

A loud noise caused him to break off what he was about to say. They looked up the hill. She gasped. A farm tractor was barreling down the hill toward them. There was no one in the driver's seat.

Isaac grabbed her hand and pulled her away from the buggy. They ran to safety, then turned to watch in horror as the tractor slammed into the buggy, smashing through it. It hit the guardrail and stopped. Isaac approached it carefully, vaulting up on the still-churning tractor and killing the engine.

The look on his face told her that he didn't believe this was an accident.

FOURTEEN

She was still shaking an hour later when she thought of their near miss.

"Are we returning to Waylan Grove?" she asked after Isaac got off the phone with his chief.

He shook his head. "I called the chief. She said that someone they believe is Zave has been spotted several times in the past three days. He can't be there and here. As much as I don't want to believe it, it may be that the tractor accident was just that. An accident."

The skepticism in his voice echoed the doubt in her own mind. However, hearing that Zave had been seen not once but several times made her question herself.

"I find it hard to believe it was an accident. Even though I know such things happen. They can't all be brought on by someone wishing to hurt someone else."

"There is that." He pivoted to face her. They were standing in the barn, the only place they could be assured of finding five minutes of privacy. She knew that they shouldn't be out here alone, but they had come so close to dying that she agreed to go with him when he asked her if he could speak with her for a few minutes. She knew she'd have some explaining to do. His clenched jaw told her that while he had been scared, he was also a little bit upset with her choice to leave the property. Well, that decision couldn't be undone. And she still felt that she had no choice. She had chosen to be a midwife, and that meant to assist women in their time of need.

"I can't understand why you left the property." She flinched at his harsh tone. He sighed and reached out and pulled her close. She let him. They both needed some comfort, she thought. She leaned her head against his chest, closing her eyes and listening to the steady thump of his heartbeat. He smelled of soap and hard work. It was a comforting scent, one that made her feel safe and loved.

Loved? Her eyes popped open. Oh, no. She couldn't go there.

But it was too late. She knew that she loved him. And soon, she would leave him. Her heart cracked inside at the revelation, knowing their story would not have a happy ending.

"I didn't mean to yell," he murmured, his chest vibrating under her cheek as he spoke. "Liz, when I realized you were gone, I thought my heart would stop. I have never harnessed a horse to a buggy that quickly. I know that I drove the poor animal faster than I ought to have."

"What happened with the wheel?" She should move back, she thought. But she remained where she was.

This might be her last private moment with him. What was the harm?

A soft chuckle erupted from him. "I can't believe how little sense I showed. I would have lectured Mary if I had seen her drive the buggy the way I did. There was a pothole, Lizzy. A deep crater of a pothole the size of Lake Erie, and I was so worried I didn't even see the thing."

She winced. He wasn't blaming her, she could hear that. He was merely relating the story now. Still, guilt gnawed at her.

"The moment the buggy bounced, I knew what I had done. It came down so hard, and I heard a crack as it broke. At least it was the buggy. The horse might have been hurt had he stepped wrong in that hole."

She would have felt horrible if the beautiful animal had suffered because Isaac was trying to find her. Thankfully, no one had been injured. She would not have to carry that burden.

Lifting her head away from his chest, she raised her eyes to gaze at his face. "I didn't mean to cause trouble. But the woman, she was having a difficult labor. I'm a midwife, Isaac. How could I ignore her distress? What if something had gone wrong with the birth? There were three lives at stake."

"Three?"

The first smile since the accident burst from her. The afternoon had been harrowing, but there had been joy, as well. "Yes, three. She had twins. Two gorgeous boys, who had very strong lungs."

Both boys had been wailing when she'd left the house. It was a beautiful sound. The sound of new life.

He grinned back. When their eyes held, the smiles faded from both faces.

Longing grew.

"I came so close to failing you today."

What?

"How do you figure that? I made my own choice."

He nodded slowly. "That you did. And I understand it, even if I can't say I like it. But I made you a promise. I meant it, too. I will protect you. I will see that you are safe."

She blinked to clear her eyes. He was such a dear man.

"Sorry I'm not making your promise easy to keep."

He didn't respond for a long moment. "Lizzy Miller, I really want to kiss you."

She trembled. She couldn't answer him.

Apparently, he took her lack of answer for approval. His head moved toward her. She could have moved away. Probably she should have. She didn't, though. Instead, she held her breath as his lips brushed hers softly. It was exquisite, the tender feel of his kiss.

When he kissed her a second time, she followed his lead and kissed him back. She'd never been kissed by a man before. She knew in her heart she might never be kissed again.

When he lifted his head and searched her face, his gaze worried, she knew that she did love Isaac Yoder. He might not love her. Nor was he planning on joining the Amish church again. These two kisses would have to last in her memory for a very long time.

"Don't say you're sorry," she begged when he opened his mouth to speak. "I'm not sorry. I know we don't have a future together. I'm not expecting anything from you."

A shadow fell over his face. He stroked her cheek once, then dropped his arms from her. "I shouldn't have kissed you."

She snorted. "I kissed you back."

She moved away from him. "We shouldn't be out here alone. I won't leave the property again without telling you."

She turned on her heel and marched briskly back to the house, aching as she left her heart behind with a man who didn't want it enough to leave the *Englisch* world.

Isaac remained in the barn after she had stalked away. He needed time to process all that had happened and to figure out his next move. Falling in love had never been on his radar. Falling in love with a sweet and sassy Amish girl was something that he would have never chosen, not in a million years. Remembering their kiss, his pulse hitched. How could he not love her? She was gentle but strong, and the way she cared for others made him admire her even when he was ready to knock his head against a proverbial wall because she didn't take her own safety into account.

He had an idea that she had strong feelings for him,

too. The way she'd kissed him back, and the sorrow in her blue eyes, said as much.

But the matter stood that they were still from two different worlds, and that wasn't likely to change.

A heavy sigh left him, the air whooshing from him in a cleansing surge. He couldn't stand here all day.

Lily barked. Not a frenzied bark of trouble, but a welcoming bark. Frowning, he hastily left the barn. A police cruiser sat in the driveway. He grinned and strode to where a familiar face was waiting for him.

Ryder was standing on the front porch, his customary grin spread across his face. Isaac's adrenaline spiked. If Ryder was here, that must mean there had been a development in the case.

"Ryder, what's up? I'm assuming you're not here for a casual visit."

Ryder laughed, but his eyes gleamed. "You'd be right. The search warrant came through. I figured that since you have now actually seen Zave for yourself, it would be a good idea if you accompanied me. You in?"

Excitement started to roll through him. They were starting to get somewhere.

"Absolutely, I'm in! Hold on." Dashing back through the house, he found his *mamm* and Lizzy in the kitchen. "Lizzy, can I talk with you for a moment?"

She set the plate she was cleaning down and followed him through the house and out onto the porch. Her eyes widened and she smiled when she saw their guest.

"Ryder! How lovely to see you."

Ryder grinned and Isaac rolled his eyes. His friend flirted too much.

"Same goes, Lizzy. I just came to steal Isaac for a bit."

"Oh? Where are you off to?"

He gestured to Ryder. "The search warrant came in. We're going to go check on it. Oh, wait." He turned to Ryder in consternation. "I don't want to leave Lizzy here." He brought Ryder up to speed. The other man whistled.

"Sounds like you have had an exciting time."

That was one way to put it.

Ryder waved his hand. "Don't worry. The chief called the police here. One of the officers will be driving by the house on a regular basis. If he sees any cars, or if something seems out of place, he'll check it out."

"Go," Lizzy urged. "I will use your phone if I need help. You need to solve this case."

Without thinking, he leaned in and kissed her cheek. "Stay in the house and keep Lily close. I will be back as soon as I take care of this."

He ignored Ryder's raised eyebrows as he got into the cruiser.

"Dude, I've never even seen you flirt before. I can't believe you kissed her!" Ryder knew him too well.

"It was a peck on the cheek. Nothing to get worked up about." He tried to shrug it off.

Ryder wasn't buying it. "I'd accept that from most guys. Not from you. If Isaac Yoder kisses a woman, it means something."

He sighed. This might be a long day. "Just drop it, Ryder, okay?"

"I'm just saying."

He threw a glare at his best friend.

"Fine, I'll drop it. But I won't forget it."

Yeah, he didn't doubt that.

They stopped by the police station long enough for Isaac to put his police uniform on. Then they hopped in Ryder's car and were off to the restaurant. The moment the owner saw them enter, his face darkened to an alarming shade of red.

"I won't have it!" he bellowed. "I'm a respectable businessman. I pay my taxes on time. You have no right to be here harassing me and scaring away my customers."

"What customers?" Ryder scoffed.

There were two people sitting at a table, and they both had uniforms on.

"It's the slow time of day. They'll start arriving soon."

Isaac let Ryder handle the "respectable businessman." He held in his snort. In his experience, respectable businessmen did not consort with drug dealers and murderers.

"We have a warrant to search your restaurant." Ryder pulled out the warrant the judge had signed.

The owner's red face paled so fast Isaac thought he'd faint at their feet. He made a few more token protests, but it was clear that he knew there was nothing he could do to stop them.

Isaac walked to the door and flipped the sign to

Closed and twisted the lock. "No one comes in while we are conducting the search." The owner sank down into a chair, shaking and wringing his hands.

Isaac and Ryder began their search, working their way methodically through the restaurant. They tried to do it with as little damage to the premises as possible. Searches could be devastating if they got out of hand.

He pulled some books off a shelf. He opened one. It was an album filled with newspaper clippings. One of them caught his eye, but it took him a few seconds to figure out what it was that got his attention. When he saw it, he bellowed for Ryder. "I got something."

Ryder rushed over to see it. Isaac pointed to the bakery on the picture. "What does that look like to you?"

Ryder narrowed his eyes. Then they widened. "That's the logo!"

The logo from Bill's hat. So now they knew where to go to get more information about what kind of a person Bill was. Maybe they'd even discover who his friends and contacts were. It was also possible they might get a lead to help them locate Sue.

"You got to see what I found."

Isaac took the article and pocketed it before he followed Ryder to the back office. There were several pictures on the owner's desk. Pictures of Isaac with Lizzy. He shook his head amazed. The owner didn't look like one to take pictures or stalk people. Ryder pointed at a picture on the wall. It was the owner, and his arm was slung around the shoulders of a scowling young man. Zave.

Isaac pulled it down off the wall and carried it and

the photos to the owner. The man was sweating. His shoulders sagged. He'd given up.

"He's my stepson, Xavier."

Xavier, Zave. Got it.

"Where'd you get these?" Isaac indicated the photos.

"Please, he's had a hard life." When the man could see they wouldn't budge, he answered. "He had a, um, colleague following you."

Isaac narrowed his eyes at the man. "When you say colleague, what kind of occupation are you talking about?"

The owner didn't respond, but instead shoved his hands into his pocket and shifted his gaze away from Isaac.

"Just what kind of work was your stepson involved in, anyway?" Ryder didn't shout, but the man flinched at his cold voice.

"Like I said, he's had a hard life—"

"We know he's dealing drugs," Isaac stated, even though they had no actual proof. The owner sighed and hung his head. "I'm going to assume that the guy following us is also a dealer."

The owner nodded, head still down.

Great. Followed by two drug dealers. "He lost sight of you several days ago. But he's still looking. He says you're trying to destroy his life," the restaurant owner said.

"Sir." Isaac held on to his temper. "Your stepson is wanted for murder. I am going to have you brought in to the station for further questioning."

When the man opened his mouth to protest, Isaac

stopped him with a glare. "Don't. Right now, you're facing possible charges of aiding and abetting a criminal." Isaac read the man his rights and called for a car to come and transport the man to the station. He'd let him wait for a few hours before he went in to question him.

The moment they were back in the car, Isaac pulled out his phone. "I need to have Jill or Keith stop by my house and tell Lizzy and my mom what's going on. They need to know that we're following a lead and might be later than planned. Also, Lizzy might think of something if she gets more details."

"We're going to LaMar Pond, then?"

"Yep. We have a bakery to visit. I'm pretty sure Bill worked there. Now that we know for sure that Zave was dealing drugs, I think we need proof that Bill was in the drug business." He shot Ryder a glance. "I'm wondering if the bakery sold more than pastries."

FIFTEEN

Where was Isaac? Lizzy tried to tamp down the impatience brewing inside her. She knew that Isaac was checking on a lead. He had told her to stay in the house, and she would, but it was making her crazy waiting for him, not knowing what was happening outside his mother's house.

"Lizzy," his mother murmured. "It will be well. *Gott* is protecting my son."

She turned and considered the woman comfortably kneading the dough that she had made that morning. Lizzy had seen her own mother do the same task countless times and knew that the bread served that evening at dinner would be heavy and flavorful, just right for dipping in soup or slathering with homemade jam. Ruth Yoder didn't appear to be anxious for her son. How could that be? Lizzy bit back the question. Isaac had abandoned the Amish church, had left the Plain world and had become a police officer, despite his family's desires. She understood the reasons, and her heart ached for the sorrow the death of Joshua had caused the family.

Still, to watch Ruth, one would never know that her heart had been broken, to lose two of her sons, as she must have felt she had.

Sighing, she continued the task of cutting up the vegetables that Ruth had given her. Lizzy was only too glad to have something to occupy her mind with, but she still found her thoughts wandering.

Finally, she couldn't stand it. "How can you be so calm when your son has left the church and is doing such a dangerous job?" She bit her lip, the sound of her voice echoing loudly in the room. Wooden floors do nothing to absorb the sounds the way carpeting would.

"I trust *Gott*," the woman explained, her voice as unruffled as before. Her eyes, though, glinted with a sliver of silent pain. Lizzy was ashamed for her outburst. Ruth wasn't done, however. "Lizzy, the circumstances surrounding my Joshua's death wounded Isaac deeply. We were all wounded. My husband, he struggled for the first time in his life about whether or not to go to the *Englisch* law, but in the end, decided that he would follow our bishop's decision. Isaac, as you know, did not agree. They fought, and for a long time, Isaac and my husband had bitter feelings between them. My husband forgave Isaac, but he died before Isaac could learn of this. I have told him. And I have seen his faith beginning to awaken again. I believe that he will return. It is my comfort."

Gathering the vegetables she had chopped, Lizzy pondered her hostess's words. Would Isaac return to his faith? She prayed he would. Heat pooled in her cheeks as she considered the possibility of what their relationship could become if that happened. Could she allow herself to act on the love growing in her heart? She trusted Isaac in a way she had not been able to trust any man since Chad Weller had devastated her life. But all of her dreams meant nothing if Isaac didn't return. A hint of an idea of leaving the Plain community to stay with him touched the edges of her mind, but she shoved it aside. Her life was in the Amish community, regardless of his decision. No human attachment could ever take precedence over God.

So for now, any dreams of a life with Isaac Yoder had to be buried.

"Lizzy," Isaac's sister said, entering the room. "You have visitors."

Visitors? Who would be visiting her? The girl wouldn't announce Isaac that way. Maybe, her heart pounded, maybe it was other officers with news. Bad or good, she couldn't begin to guess.

Wiping her hands on a towel, she straightened her *kapp*, and swiftly moved out to the open living room area, the heels of her plain black boots clattering on the polished shine of the hardwood floors. Seeing the familiar face standing in the entranceway, her jaw dropped in shock.

The young woman must have felt the vibrations of the floor because she turned at Lizzy's approach, and Lizzy knew for a fact that the other woman would not have heard her. Rebecca grinned at her younger sister; her blue eyes, the same color as Lizzy's, sparkled with pleasure. Lizzy knew that people thought the sisters looked alike. In fact, before Rebecca had left the Plain community, they had received many comments on how similar they were.

"Rebecca!" Lizzy greeted her sister, instinctively signing even as she said her name verbally. She was a bit unsettled seeing her beautiful older sister now, when danger lurked everywhere she turned. "What are you doing here?"

Rebecca grinned at her sister and pushed her blond braid over her shoulder.

"Miles is still at a trial in Ohio, so he dropped me off to visit Addie," Rebecca signed in her flowing ASL. "I was disappointed that you weren't there, but I ran into Sue, our old driver, and she said you were visiting friends here, and since she was coming this way, she would give me a ride."

Lizzy tilted her head and looked over her sister's shoulder at her driver and friend. Her friend who had been missing, and whom she had thought was dead. Unease slithered through her gut, like thick grease churning. Where had Sue been all this time? And how had Sue known she was here? She had never told her. The last time she had talked with Sue, the woman had been brokenhearted over the death of her brother, Bill. Now, she was wearing a smile.

Not her regular smile. This smile was cold and had the flavor of contempt in the slight curl of her upper lip. Uncomfortable, she slid her eyes away from Sue's. And her gaze fell on the logo in the upper left corner of Sue's button-down green collared shirt. It was her work shirt. Lizzy remembered Sue saying that she worked part-time for a bakery. She'd never paid attention to the name of the bakery before. She should have. Lizzy swallowed. In her mind, she recalled Jill and Keith stopping by earlier and explaining Isaac's theory that the bakery that Bill had been working for may have fronted a drug-running business. She couldn't believe that she had forgotten that Sue also worked for a bakery. Was it possible that her friend was also involved in dealing drugs?

Her gut said she was. The woman standing confidently before her, eyes cold as an arctic wind, was not the sweet person she had known.

How she knew, she couldn't have said, but at that moment, Lizzy was absolutely certain that Sue had been working with Bill. She could detect no hint of mourning or sorrow in her sneering face. No, the doting older sister was gone.

And suddenly, Lizzy had a horrible thought. What if Sue had not had food poisoning? What if she had intentionally set up her brother to get killed? Could she have been so greedy that she had eliminated her brother and planned her own disappearance?

"I see you're starting to figure things out," Sue said, her voice calm. Except she had reached into the bag she carried and had jerked out a gun. A gun she had even now shoved in Rebecca's side. Rebecca's eyes widened, the color leaching from her face. Lizzy hated seeing her sister's fear, knowing that Rebecca, like her, had horrors in her past from being held captive by a killer, not once, but twice. Rebecca surprised her, though. Outside of paling, she showed no reaction. Her eyes hardened and she gazed at Lizzy, before dropping her glance to her left hand, held against her stomach.

Discreetly, Lizzy slid her glance to her sister's hand.

"Watch. Wait. Plan." Her sister's fingers flashed as she quickly fingerspelled the three simple words. Lizzy understood the message. Their goal was to survive and watch for an opportunity to move.

She would do that, but if the woman made a move to shoot or hurt her sister, all plans of waiting would be canceled. Lizzy had every intention of getting her beloved sister safely back to her husband and her baby.

Please, God, please save us. Let Isaac find us in time.

"Why don't we take a walk outside. I think we have some things to discuss and it's a lovely day."

Lizzy clearly heard the threat in Sue's casual comments. If they had stayed in the house, Isaac's sister and mother would have been in danger. She couldn't be responsible for them getting hurt. She nodded, then signed to Rebecca, being sure to voice her words so Sue wouldn't think she was being sneaky. "We're going outside."

Sue indicated with the gun that they should head toward her car. She forced Rebecca to get into the backseat, and had Lizzy tie her sister's hands. Tears spurted to her eyes as she complied, effectively shutting off conversation with her sister. Not that they would be allowed to continue to fingerspell or sign with each other.

Lizzy could hear Lily barking in the house. She slid into the passenger's seat at Sue's prompting. Sue immediately took out a nylon rope and bound Lizzy's hands. She connected the rope to Lizzy's ankle, hindering the freedom of her motions. She couldn't even reach the phone in her pocket.

Silently, Sue folded her body behind the steering wheel and slammed the door. Her jaw was hard as she began to drive.

Lizzy didn't want to encourage her to use her gun, but she also wondered if she could talk Sue into giving them information that they could use.

"Sue—" she began, but halted as the gun swung in her direction.

"Don't tempt me, Amish girl. You are not my favorite person at the moment."

Lizzy swallowed down the questions burning inside her brain.

Again, she sent up a silent prayer for Isaac to find them. In the meantime, she needed to stay sharp. If he didn't arrive, she would have to save them.

At the moment, however, doubt and fear had melded into a heavy weight in her gut. If nothing changed, she and her sister were going to die.

Isaac and Ryder stepped out of the police cruiser and looked at the pristine faux marble edifice standing before them. It was the most out of place structure Isaac had ever seen.

Ryder whistled. "Did any planning about fitting in with the locale go into this place?" Ryder muttered, awe and disbelief coloring his voice.

Isaac narrowed his eyes, taking in the fancy burgundy-and-gold awning. "Apparently not."

The sign swung from gold chains above the door. Mario's Italian Bakery, the sign read. Except that they had looked into the owner of this business, and it wasn't Mario. In fact, no Mario had ever owned or been employed on these premises, according to the official records. Oh, well. No law against that. He just thought it was odd. The owner, in fact, had been a man named Frank, until last year. Frank had left the place to his niece, Teresa. But as yet, Teresa had been a very hands-off owner. The young man he had talked with on the phone had never even seen her, and didn't think anyone else had, either.

"Don't you think it's odd that no one here has ever seen the new owner?" he asked Ryder as they waited for the two cars at the intersection to crawl on by before they crossed the street and made their way to the bakery.

"Sure do. Especially seeing as her uncle practically lived on the premises. Apparently, she left a man named Chris to be her eyes and ears in the place." Ryder consulted his notes. "Chris has checked out okay. He has no outstanding warrants. He is divorced, but pays child support regularly and on time. By all accounts, he is a devoted father, and a fair manager. His only brush with the law has been two speeding tickets, both of which he fought in court. The one he won, the other he didn't."

"So, a regular guy, but we're looking into him, anyway." Isaac nodded to himself as he filed all the information away.

"Yeah. 'Cause he might look clean, but one of the

men under his management was a drug dealer, murdered in a drug transaction gone bad. How could he not know that? Why would he hire the man?"

Good question. Isaac opened the bakery door, then stepped back to allow the harried woman with a bag of fragrant baked goods in one arm and a screaming toddler tugging at her other hand to exit. She smiled briefly in thanks before continuing down the street, talking to her child in a stern voice all the way.

Ryder gave a mock shudder. Isaac smirked at him. "You're not fooling me, my friend. I've seen the way the kids love you."

Ryder gave him a hard glare. "They might love me, but I am not father material, buddy. Don't even go there."

Whoa. He'd hit a nerve. Obviously, there was some baggage that Ryder had hidden in his past. However, considering the things he himself had carried around for the last seven years, he wasn't about to pry. He still couldn't believe he'd told Lizzy about his *dat* and Joshua.

He couldn't let himself think of the pretty blonde right now. He needed to focus so he could get her out of danger. And so he could get out of her life, hopefully with minimal scars on his heart. She tugged at his emotions way too much for his comfort.

He could go back to the Amish culture. Okay, where had that thought come from? He had no intention of going back. True, his relationship with God was growing stronger. And he believed his *mamm* that his *dat* had forgiven him before he'd died. But his life was here, in the *Englisch* world. And he was doing a necessary service in this job, although lately, the badge didn't fit so comfortably. It almost felt like he was playing a role.

And, he had to admit, if he was Amish, he could court Lizzy.

Maybe she would—

He stopped that thought before it fully formed. There was no way he would ever ask her to leave her church. Lizzy was Amish, clean through to her bones. Even though her sister had found her place in the *Englisch* world, Lizzy never would. Not to mention that, now, if she did decide to leave, she would be shunned and lose her whole family. Something neither he nor Rebecca had had to deal with because they'd never been baptized.

He brought himself back to the present and followed Ryder over to the register in the corner. A polished man with dark red hair and a sincere smile waited. Unlike the other employees, this man wore a crisp white shirt with a solid dark blue tie. Chris.

"May I help you, Officers?" Chris asked. His voice was unhurried. Isaac thought he detected a bit of a Pittsburgh accent in the way the man formed his *o*'s.

"Actually, Chris, we were hoping to speak with you for a moment," Isaac responded.

Over his shoulder, Chris called for one of the employees to come and man the front of the bakery. Within seconds, a young woman came to replace him. Chris opened up the gate leading to the back. "Come, and we can sit in the privacy of my office."

Soon, they were ensconced in wooden folding chairs in front of Chris's rather modest office desk. Isaac looked around the room, somewhat surprised at the lack of pomp in the room. Seeing the ostentatious front of the building, he had expected the inside to be more or less the same. Chris extended the hospitality of offering to get them a drink of water, or perhaps coffee or tea, which both officers declined. Isaac was itching to do this interview and find the next clue to bring them closer to the ringleader.

He opened his notepad to begin the questioning. "Chris, we're looking into some unsavory dealings with some of your employees."

A grimace crossed the manager's face. "You might as well say it. You're here about what happened with Bill. I've been expecting you."

The two officers exchanged a glance. "Yes, we are here about him," Ryder confirmed. "I am curious why you were willing to hire him, given his past."

A red flush crept up Chris's face and clashed with his red hair. "It was an emotional decision, one I have regretted almost since it was made. One of the other workers here, Sue, is his sister. We were dating at the time, and she told me to hire him. I didn't want to, because I knew he was bad news and wasn't a good investment, but she insisted. I was right, which gave me no pleasure, but by that time, we had broken up, so I will admit to feeling a little vindictive when I told her I was letting him go."

Isaac frowned. "I spoke to Sue on the phone to tell her about her brother's death. She had seemed pretty broken up about it, but not once did she indicate that she was working for the same business as Bill had. Then she disappeared."

His instincts went on alert as the other man hesitated. Leaning forward, he pinned the manager with a glare. "Do not lie to us, Chris. You don't want to face an obstruction of justice charge."

The manager slumped in his chair, running a hand that shook slightly through his red hair.

"She's not listed as an employee here. Sue Allister is not her full name. Her full name is Teresa Susanne Allister Bailey."

Teresa Bailey. The unseen owner of the company.

The hair on his arms stood as several pieces came together in his mind. Sue, or Teresa, had incredible access to the bakery without really registering. She was unlisted as an employee, but the other employees might not have known that. And her business as a driver for the Amish gave her reasons to travel to various places without raising suspicions.

Sue had forced Chris to hire her brother with drug connections. And Sue had tasked her brother with making the run that had proven to be fatal to him. Had she done so on purpose? Had she planned for him to be killed?

"Why were you letting him go?" Ryder interrupted his musing.

"He had been seen doing a drug interaction on the bakery premises."

"In other words, he endangered your business with the possibility of bringing the police in." Isaac heard the irony in his voice, as the police were indeed brought in.

"Yes, Officer. I have done my best to run a good business and have continued to build the strong reputation that Frank had fostered before his passing. I knew that if Bill remained, sooner or later that reputation would come under scrutiny and be tarnished. I told Sue that I would quit rather than keep him on. She agreed and told me she'd handle it. But he had gotten himself killed first."

No, he hadn't. Isaac knew with absolute clarity that his sister had done just as she had promised. He suspected that Chris knew nothing about the discreet drug trade the owner of the bakery had been doing behind his back.

"And how is your business running with its owner missing?"

He narrowed his eyes as Chris swallowed.

"Don't start lying to me now, Chris."

Chris sighed and bowed his head, giving up. "She's not missing. She said she needed to disappear for a few days, but that she would keep in contact. When I heard her place was trashed, I thought she'd known someone wanted to hurt her. When she called me, I told her about her place. It didn't seem to faze her in the least."

Of course it hadn't; Isaac kept the sneer off his face with effort. It seemed Sue had been two steps ahead of them the entire time. Isaac had no doubt she'd been responsible for her apartment being trashed.

Another thought had him leaping from his chair. He had wondered how Lizzy had been found at the motel. It had to have been Sue. He recalled Lizzy telling her she could identify Bill's shooter. If Sue was involved in her brother's death, as he was sure she was, Lizzy was a definite threat to her. He suspected that Sue had been connected with the attacks on Lizzy. She had driven to Ohio with Lizzy enough to be familiar with the area, not to mention the fact that she knew what Lizzy looked like.

"Thank you for your time, Chris. We'll be in touch if we need anything else."

He all but ran from the bakery, ignoring Ryder's astonished expression. His friend was right behind him, but the moment they were sitting in the cruiser, Ryder's curiosity burst forth.

"What was that all about?"

Isaac waited impatiently for his friend to get behind the wheel. "Sue is behind the drug ring."

"I got that."

"When Lizzy talked with her after Bill's death, she told Sue that she could identify the killer. I think that Sue and Zave were working together."

Understanding and consternation vied for possession on Ryder's face. "Sue couldn't have been pleased with that."

"Exactly. I expect she was all about keeping Lizzy from identifying him. Remember, the attacks started right after that. She knows who I am, which means she can find Lizzy."

Ryder immediately jerked the car into Drive and pulled away from the curb. He flipped on the lights for good measure.

They didn't even stop by the station. There was no time. Ryder drove to Isaac's mother's house as fast as he could safely manage it. Isaac waited for his friend to throw the car into Park, then he jumped out and raced up the steps, Ryder at his heels. The two men burst into the house, startling a shriek from his mother.

"*Mamm!* Where is Lizzy?"

Please let her be here.

His mother's face, though, told him that he was too late. "I don't know, Isaac. Lizzy's sister came to visit with another woman. They stepped outside, and then they were gone."

Isaac felt as if the wind had been knocked out of him. He had failed to protect Lizzy. He had promised her he would keep her safe, but he hadn't even recognized the danger when it had stood right in front of them.

"Isaac, what can we do?"

He would not give up. He would find Lizzy and her sister and get them home, or die trying. "I need anything you can give me about the car they were driving. I need to give the dispatcher something to pass on." A BOLO, or a Be On the Look Out alert, was going to be his quickest way to get the news out.

Ruth Yoder called Isaac's sister, Mary, in. Mary was able to give him a description of the car, for which he was intensely grateful. As soon as they had the description, Ryder rushed back to the car to issue the alert.

"Is there anything else you need?"

Isaac paused at the door to look over his shoulder at his mother.

"Pray, *Mamm.* Pray."

SIXTEEN

The sky was darkening when Sue pulled the car to a stop in front of a place that Lizzy recognized all too well. The abandoned building where Bill had been shot less than a week ago. She had thought she'd never see this place again, and she certainly had never imagined being brought back by a woman she'd considered a friend holding her at gunpoint.

"Why are you doing this, Sue?" she whispered.

Sue was searching the edges of the lot. She ignored Lizzy's question at first, then her mouth lifted in a satisfied smile.

"I couldn't let you identify him." She jerked her chin to the north side of the lot.

Lizzy's eyes shot in the direction indicated, and she gasped. Sauntering toward them was the man who had shot and killed Bill. At Sue's chuckle, she shivered as it flowed over her like a bucket of ice water.

"He killed your brother!" she choked out, horrified.

"Yes, he did. At my orders." She sneered at Lizzy. "My brother had wasted the opportunity I had given him. Our uncle had left me the bakery." She flicked her fingers lazily at the logo on her shirt. "It was the perfect cover-up for the operation I ran. Bill had somehow gotten wind of it, and he wanted a cut. I told him not to cross me, and he promised to toe the line and keep himself off the radar. The fool couldn't even handle it. Then he thought he'd cheat me by trying to cut deals on my property. When he met Zave there, though, he was supposed to make sure there were no witnesses to his death."

She had seen it, though. Why had Sue let her live?

Abruptly, Sue unlatched her seat belt and exited the car. Lizzy tugged at the ropes holding her wrists together, and she felt the nylon shift. Had it loosened? She couldn't be sure. If it had, it still wasn't enough for her to get herself free. Fear skittered through her whole system. A quick glance up told her that Sue and the man were still occupied talking. Actually, it seemed as though they were arguing. Hopefully, they would argue long enough for her to make some headway on her ropes.

She desperately wished she could find some way to reassure Rebecca. Even if she could turn and face her sister, she knew her sister did not read lips, so there was nothing she could say to her without the ability to move her hands. From the backseat, she could hear a flurry of movement, which let her know that Rebecca was also working on her bindings. Rebecca was not one to quit. She had fought for her life, and had too much to lose now to give up.

Isaac's face came to her mind. She had not told him

that she was falling in love with him. If she ever saw him again… No. Even then, she would have to keep those feelings secret. Because it would not be fair to burden him, to make him feel pressured to choose her and the Amish faith.

Would he choose it on his own?

It didn't matter right now. Nothing mattered except finding a way out of this horrible situation. She refocused on the task of freeing her hands, furiously working on the nylon ropes. So intent was she on her business that she started when the driver's door opened again.

"I figured you'd be trying to get free," Sue said, amused. "It's no use, Lizzy. You're stuck right where I put you, but don't worry, I don't plan on leaving you in the car."

The passenger's side door next to her opened. Horror clawed through her as the man she'd watched shoot a man in cold blood bent to pick her up out of the car. Lizzy fought as best she could, trying to kick out with her legs. He merely laughed.

"You keep fighting, and I will shoot Rebecca."

Sue's words stopped her movements. Rebecca! Lizzy was able to twist her head around enough to see that Sue had pulled her sister from the car and was again holding a gun to her. Lizzy had no choice. There was not a single doubt in her mind that Sue would shoot Rebecca like she promised. She'd probably shoot them both soon. If she'd have her own brother killed, she'd probably be willing to kill anyone. But Lizzy wasn't going to make it happen any sooner, not if she could help it.

The two women were brought inside the old building. The dank scent of mold and rotting wood, accompanied by some scents that Lizzy would prefer not to identify, assaulted her senses. She gagged, causing Sue to laugh harshly. The man carrying her, however, wasn't amused.

The light filtering in from the single window was dim. Sue's face was in shadows. The jolting motion of being carried was making Lizzy's already stressed-out stomach churn. She gagged again, and choked back the bile that threatened to rise.

"You throw up on me and I'll make you regret it," he growled.

She gulped in the dirty air through her mouth, hoping that smelling it less would quell some of the nausea roiling in her stomach. Behind her, she heard Rebecca gag and retch. A slap followed the sound, and she cringed to hear her sister gasp.

Lizzy bit the inside of her cheek to help her keep her silence. The tinny flavor of blood filled her mouth. *God, please help us be strong. Be with us. Protect us.* She kept the litany of silent prayer running as she was carried back, deeper into the bowels of the wrecked building. The scuffling of steps behind told her that Sue was bringing Rebecca along, as well.

The room they were led to was dark. A single window high up on the wall was the only source of light. The fading sunlight cast a dim ray into the room, barely cutting a slice through the shadows. Soon, she knew, even that light would be gone. Sue and the man's faces were in shadows.

"Zave, set her down over there," Sue ordered.

Zave set her down on the floor hard enough to jostle her bones. She hissed as her head bumped the wall behind her. Sue pushed Rebecca down beside her. At least they had enough mobility to reach and grab each other's hands. It was an uncomfortable position, and Lizzy winced as her leg was twisted at an unnatural angle. She couldn't bring herself to let go of her sister. Rebecca's grip on her hands intensified. This had to be even more terrifying for her deaf sister, unable to even hear what was going on.

Keeping her gaze locked on Sue, she saw the woman lift something and place it on a table on the other side of the room. A single click, shockingly loud, and then light flared upward into the room. Sue had some sort of lantern in the room.

She had prepared a space for this purpose. Never would Lizzy have believed the woman to be so cold-blooded as to plan the atrocities she now knew she had committed. And continued to commit.

She picked up the gun that was lying on the table next to the light. This was it. Lizzy tightened her grip on her sister's hand, trying to tell her through her touch that she loved her. Tears tracked from her eyes, and she knew without looking that Rebecca was weeping softly beside her. Whirling to face them, Sue held the gun steady, a malicious smirk on her face.

"I have not worked so hard for anyone to take what I've built from me. Not anyone."

Without warning, she turned the gun on Zave and fired. It was so fast Lizzy didn't even have time to blink.

The man gaped at Sue as his body slid down the wall. He was still alive. She could hear his gasping breaths.

"Why?" he choked.

Sue took a step toward him. "You failed me, Zave. You bungled the whole affair, and then didn't get rid of the witness. Because of your failure, she was able to go to the police. And she would be able to identify you. I knew that she had to be taken care of. But you have become a liability, as well. It would have been too time-consuming and risky to do the job one at a time. It might also have led the police to me. This way, I will eliminate all the loose ends. This building will be torched, and no one will connect it to me.

"Goodbye."

Lizzy must have had her phone on her. The signal from the phone was moving, allowing the cops to follow it and zero in on where they were heading.

"The car was spotted entering the Carstairs place ten minutes ago."

Isaac listened to the dispatcher's voice, relief and dread mingling. A lot could happen in ten minutes. He jabbed a trembling finger at the button to respond. "We're on our way," he yelled into the microphone. "Car six is en route and will be on scene in five minutes."

Or less, if he could help it.

"Ryder, we need to move."

Nodding, his face grim, Ryder hit the sirens and shoved his foot down hard on the gas. The cruiser jolted forward, engine revving as it roared past the cars pulling to the side of the road. Isaac sat beside him, hands fisted. It was no time for jokes or pleasant conversation. Two women were in mortal danger. A thought occurred to him.

"Rebecca's husband is in the area. I'm going to contact him and let him know our location."

A minute later, he disconnected his phone. "Done. Miles Olsen is en route, even as we speak. Lieutenant Anderson is bringing him along."

The drive to the Carstairs place was just up ahead. Ryder steered the car into the parking lot. Isaac kept his eyes moving, scanning the area. The car that his sister had said Lizzy's sister arrived in when she came to visit his *mamm*'s house was there. Another car was also there.

Ryder radioed in the other license plate. "Xavier Daniels," he reported back.

Isaac's eyes widened. Xavier Daniels had been in and out of the prison system since he turned sixteen.

Weapons out and at the ready, the two men approached the building. "We're on scene and entering the building," Isaac said softly into the radio hooked to his shoulder. They eased through the opening in the front door, then paused, listening. No sounds. Keeping their steps as quiet as possible, they entered, peering around the corners.

A sudden shot rang out from the back of the building. "Shots fired!" Isaac snapped into his radio. Then he and Ryder were moving back in the direction they'd heard the shot. His blood was pounding in his veins and his gut clenched. He pushed all thought of Lizzy out of his mind. If he let his emotions lead, she would die, without a doubt. Keeping a cool head was the only way he could bring her out alive.

He blocked off the thought that he might be too late. He couldn't go there.

Voices. A harsh feminine laugh. He looked back. Ryder nodded. He'd heard it, too.

They continued to make their way to the back of the building. A woman's voice pleaded. Lizzy. A surge of relief billowed up inside him. She was obviously still alive. Although she was also still stuck in the room with two killers, so they weren't out of danger yet.

The voices were coming from a room off to the left. They peered around the corner. It was clear, so they continued on. Ten seconds later, they moved into position to see into the room. Sue was right ahead of them, pointing her gun at a young man on the floor.

Xavier Daniels. He wasn't moving. Sue was still moving, though, her gun skimming over until Lizzy was in its path.

They were out of time.

"Police! Drop your weapon!" he shouted into the room.

Sue didn't drop her weapon. Instead, she whirled to point it at him. The first shot went wild. He and Ryder both dodged the bullet, and it thudded into the wall in the hallway. The raging woman made to aim again. His gun was already up, and he aimed to shoot. At the same time, Lizzy and Rebecca made an odd movement together, and Rebecca's leg kicked out, sweeping Sue's legs out from under her.

Shrieking, she dropped the gun to catch herself as she hit the ground. Before she could recover, Isaac was there, flipping her over and putting the handcuffs on her as she bucked and yelled. He raised his voice to recite her rights even as he felt the satisfying click of the handcuffs locking into place. She continued to rant as he dragged her to her feet, while avoiding her feet as she kicked out at him.

"I'll take her," Ryder said, coming up beside him. "Daniels is dead. It looks like she shot him twice. I hear sirens, hopefully the ambulance crew. I will direct them down. You see to your girl."

My girl. He wished with all his heart that was true, but knew it was an impossible dream. Still, he was so grateful she was alive. That was the most important thing. He pulled his pocketknife out, carefully sliced through the nylon bindings on Lizzy and her sister. With a cry, Lizzy lurched forward and threw her arms around his neck, weeping into his shoulder. He held her tightly, squeezing his eyes tight. He had come so close to losing her. *At least when she leaves, I'll know she's well.*

Her head lifted from his shoulder. He wanted to kiss her, but set her away from him instead. Now was definitely not the time and place for that, nor did he have that right. It hurt, but he had to keep his distance.

The sounds of voices broke into the silence. Then the sound of running feet. Miles Olsen burst into the room, his gaze skipping over everyone and zeroing in on his wife. She pushed herself off the floor and was in his arms. Miles, unlike Isaac, didn't hesitate to kiss the woman he loved.

It hit him with enough force that he rocked back on his heels. He could no longer deny it. He loved Lizzy Miller. She was the woman he had been waiting for.

And she was from the world that he had left. He couldn't have her without her world.

Which meant he had to let her go.

For the next few hours, he focused his attention on collecting statements and booking his prisoner. Lizzy and Rebecca had been unharmed, although he knew that the trials they'd been through would cause their own scars. His heart lurched. Lizzy had been through so much in her life. Would her panic attacks return?

He hurried to see her as soon as his duties were done. "Lizzy—"

She stopped him with a wide smile. "I'm fine, Isaac. I can see that you're worried about me, and yes, I will never forget this ordeal. I may even have a bad dream now and then. But, Isaac, did you see it? Rebecca and I had promised to look for any opportunity to help ourselves, and when it came, we took it. Sue would have killed us. But she didn't. You saved us, and we also saved ourselves."

He blinked. This exuberant woman was not what he expected, although he was happy to see her reacting this way.

"So, you're okay?" He thought she was, but he needed to make sure.

She nodded. "Absolutely. For the first time in a long

time, I feel like I had some control. That, and I knew that *Gott* was with us."

Yes, he thought. He felt the same way.

Grinning at the beautiful blonde beside him, he beckoned to her. "Come on. I promised to get you to your cousin's house. How about I do that?"

She nodded.

"Oh, do we need to wait for your sister?"

"No, we're leaving now." Miles and Rebecca met them in the hallway. The men watched as the sisters embraced. Miles and Isaac shook hands and Miles kissed Lizzy's cheek. Then the couple departed, Miles keeping his arm firmly around his wife's shoulders.

Isaac's throat ached. Not with jealousy. With regret. He wanted what they had, but knew that he wouldn't get it because Lizzy was the only woman he wanted it with.

Lizzy stayed with Addie for the next two weeks until her baby girl came, right on schedule. She assisted with the birth the way she'd promised, but within a day or two, she was ready to go home. Her cousin told her that she had made plans for a driver for Lizzy.

Lizzy was surprised to find Isaac waiting to drive her home in his truck. She gulped in a deep breath as she took in his familiar and beloved face. Then she frowned. Something was different. His hair. Isaac had his hair cut down to a mere half inch. The color left her face at the obvious sign that he was not even thinking of rejoining the Amish church.

"Why are you driving me home?" she asked bluntly.

Not that she wasn't happy to see him. She was. But it was also bittersweet, knowing he'd never be hers.

He shrugged. "I wanted to see you one last time. Besides, I thought you might be uncomfortable hiring an unfamiliar driver after the recent events."

And just like that, the wall of ice she had tried to build between them melted into a puddle inside her. He might have decided that they had no future, but he was still looking out for her. She would treasure this drive together, this last gift of his time and his caring, and hold it dear in her memories forever.

The drive started out uncomfortable, mostly because she was trying so hard to keep the silence from growing between them too long. Finally, he reached out and gripped her hand with his. She jumped at the unexpected contact.

"Liz, it's okay." He squeezed her hand before releasing it and putting his hand back on the wheel. "We don't need to talk the whole time. Let's just enjoy the trip. It's nice to finally be able to breathe, knowing that the bad guys have been taken care of and you are safe. I know that I'm grateful that both you and your sister are safe."

"Me, too," she whispered, her throat tight as she reflected on how close she had been to dying.

Suddenly weary, she relaxed back against the seat and closed her eyes. The swaying of the vehicle lured her into a deep sleep. When she woke up, she was startled to find that they had already entered LaMar Pond. Dismayed, she sat up straight. She had slept through most of what was likely her last time with him.

Before she knew it, they were pulling up in front of her house. *Mamm*, *Dat* and her siblings flowed out of the house and swarmed over her, exclaiming over her and touching her *kapp* to ensure her safety. *Mamm* caught her up in her arms and embraced her tightly.

"Rebecca told me about what had happened. Are you well, daughter?" Martha Miller's kind eyes searched Lizzy's face.

She cleared her throat to get rid of the constriction forming there. "I'm well, *Mamm*."

Her voice sounded like she had swallowed cotton.

Her mother gave her a gentle kiss on her forehead, then peered over her daughter's head to the police officer who had brought her little girl home.

"Officer, thank you for returning Lizzy to us. You are welcome to stay and eat dinner with us. There's plenty."

Lizzy ducked to hide her smile. There was always plenty. Her mother still cooked as though all six of her children were at home, regardless of the fact that Rebecca, Thomas and Joseph were all married and had homes and families of their own.

Her smile faded as she saw him shake his head out of the corner of her eye.

"No, thank you, ma'am. I need to be getting back to Ohio. It was a pleasure to meet you all." He nodded at Lizzy. "Lizzy."

That was going to be all the farewell she would receive. There were so many words dammed up inside her, words that she could never say with her family here. And her family was making no move to go inside and give them privacy. She understood that. Given what she had been like before she left for Ohio, they would have no way of knowing that a different Lizzy, one that had learned to love and trust, had come back to them.

"Goodbye, Isaac," she said, proud that her voice didn't shake, even though she was trembling inside. "Thank you for everything. I appreciate it."

She kept her face calm. He flashed one more quick smile at her before striding back to his car. He didn't look at her as he backed up. In seconds he was gone; the only proof that he had been there was the dust that his car had left in its wake.

SEVENTEEN

"What are you still doing here?"

Isaac glanced away from his computer screen to find Ryder hovering in the doorway. Ryder had changed out of his uniform. Isaac knew that he had plans to go and visit friends that weekend. Briefly, his eyes slid back to the document that was open on his screen. How would Ryder react when he told him what he was doing? He hadn't purposely misled his friend, but neither had he exactly openly communicated what he was thinking.

"Hey, buddy," he hedged. "I thought you left half an hour ago."

Ryder shrugged, his expression nonchalant, although his dark eyes were vivid with curiosity. "I was planning on it. I had some last-minute things that I needed to take care of. The question is, what are you doing here? I thought that you were off the clock. I saw you go out to your car."

Isaac sighed. He might as well come clean. He knew why he was hesitating. Ryder was the best friend he had ever had. While he knew he was making the right decision, he dreaded the thought that his decision might adversely affect that friendship. After all, his decision meant his whole way of life would change.

"I have decided to write my letter of resignation." He stared at the other man, trying to gauge his reaction.

Ryder's eyes popped open so wide it was amazing his eyeballs didn't fall right out of his head. "Dude, are you for real? You're quitting?"

There wasn't anything he could do to hold back the flinch at his friend's reaction. Still, it could have been worse. What he couldn't tell was if there was more than shock in Ryder's voice.

"Yes, I'm quitting. I wasn't made to be a cop, not like you are. I became a cop because I felt I had something to prove. I don't feel that way anymore. It's time I went home."

He let the silence fall between them. Hopefully, this wouldn't be a chasm they couldn't get past.

But Ryder surprised him. After his initial shocked reaction, the other man seemed to take the information in stride. In fact, Isaac was surprised to see what looked like a grin fighting to form on Ryder's face.

"I was wondering when you were going to come to your senses," Ryder remarked. All Isaac could do was stare at him. "Isaac, man, I've known for the last two months that your heart wasn't in the job. Ever since Lizzy went home you've been going through the motions, but anyone could see that you weren't happy. I will admit to wondering if you would ever go home. When I saw you at your mother's house, you just seemed to fit there, even with the urgency of the situation. Please don't take this the wrong way, but you never really fit in here. I never understood why until then."

Isaac felt as though something heavy fell from his shoulders. He hadn't realized until that moment how much he had wanted his friend to be okay with his decision.

"So, you're going to go find Lizzy, right?" Ryder raised an eyebrow and leaned his shoulder against the wall. "I mean, that is what this conversation is about, isn't it?"

Isaac was already shaking his head. "I can't go after her. Not yet."

"Why ever not?" Ryder wasn't grinning now.

"Because I have to do this for the right reasons. Lizzy is a baptized member of the Amish church. She would never agree to marry a man who wasn't Amish."

Ryder rolled his eyes, as if he wasn't even sure why they were having this conversation. "Dude, it's simple. If she needs you to be Amish again, then become Amish."

"There are things I have to do first. And I want to be sure that I can become Amish and really live that life with my whole heart. It's been seven years since I left. I have to be completely committed to that life, and to God first. Once I join the church, there's no going back."

He didn't think that would be an issue. It seemed like the past seven years had been leading up to this point. But he wasn't taking any chances. His happiness, and he thought Lizzy's, as well, relied on him making the right choice and following through with his whole heart. If he married her, but wasn't committed to the church, that would only lead to both of them suffering. He could not do that to her.

There was something else on his mind.

"If everything works out and she agrees to marry me, you'll come to the wedding, right?" he asked, serious. "If it were an *Englisch* wedding, I'd ask you to be best man, but we don't have that in Amish weddings."

"Will I be allowed?" For the first time since the conversation started, Ryder appeared hesitant. "We'll still be friends, right?"

Isaac snorted. "Idiot. Of course we'll be friends. I will need to get the bishop's permission, but outsiders attend Amish weddings all the time. You won't be able to sit with community, but you'd be there."

A smile flashed his way. "Then finish your letter and go to it. And I expect to be kept in the loop."

"That's my plan." Isaac turned back to his computer screen as the hard clatter made by Ryder's cowboy boots faded. He heard the office door open and the whisper as it swung shut. Then he shut everything out and focused on the letter that would sever his connection to the job he had held for the past few years as he searched for his place in the world. Never had he dreamed it would lead him back to his Amish roots.

Two weeks later, Isaac said his final farewells to his coworkers and headed to his apartment for the last time, to pack. It didn't take him long. By eight the next morning, he had handed in his keys.

"That's all you're taking with you?" Ryder raised a skeptical brow when Isaac tossed a single duffel bag into the bed of Ryder's pickup truck.

"Yup. I won't have much use for most of the things I owned." Isaac climbed up into the passenger seat and fastened his seat belt. "I appreciate the ride."

Ryder backed up, checking over his shoulder to make sure there was no oncoming traffic. "Not a problem. I knew you'd need someone to get you to your mother's place, seeing as you sold your truck."

Isaac had been able to sell his truck to one of the tenants at the apartment. It was amazing how freeing it had felt getting rid of most of his possessions.

He'd miss the truck, he mused. It had been convenient, but it had felt right to get rid of it.

The sun was streaming down and baking the earth when they pulled up the long winding drive that led to the old farmhouse where his mother still lived with his younger sister. She came out the door and stood on the porch when Ryder stopped his truck and stilled the engine. She'd been cooking something, probably honey biscuits. There was a smudge of flour on her left cheek.

She didn't look surprised to see him.

Suddenly, he was anxious to greet her. He stepped from the truck, and was assailed with the familiar aromas of the farm. Flowers and fresh mowed grass, baking biscuits and the cows in the field. All the scents of home.

"Mamm," he said, looking up at her. "I'd like to come back. I want to return to the Amish life."

The smile that split across her face rivaled the sun in its brilliance. She blinked her eyes. He started to smile, then realized his own vision was blurry. Any worries he might have still had about his mother's welcome were squashed as she reached out and embraced him.

Later, he went to the room where he had slept growing up. The clothes he'd worn so recently while he and Lizzy had stayed with his family were still there, waiting for him to put them on.

It felt a bit odd exchanging the blue jeans he'd grown used to for the dark trousers Amish men wore. He also had to get over the habit of reaching for his phone. He had grown very comfortable with modern technology, but he was determined to give this way of life his best shot.

His conversation with the bishop went better than he had expected.

"Your father had faith that you would return one day," the bishop told him. "He wasn't angry with you when you left. He was giving you the extra time you needed to make a decision. You were never baptized into the church. You were free to leave if that was your wish."

The bishop insisted that Isaac live with the Plain community for another season before he would agree to baptize him. Isaac didn't like it, but he understood why. The bishop wanted him to be sure. Isaac was sure, and he chafed against spending so much additional time apart from Lizzy, but he knew he had to choose this life for himself, not for her. So he agreed and tried to wait patiently.

Every night, he asked God to watch over her and keep her safe. And one day soon, he hoped to go and claim her as his bride. He just prayed she'd have him.

* * *

Six months. She hadn't seen Isaac for six months.

She knew she should give up all her hopes that he would come to find her. That would mean that he had decided to return to the Amish way of life. Something that he had been decided against doing. She knew his reasons. Isaac had so much pain stored up inside him.

Lizzy sighed and shut the door behind her, starting the trek home after helping another life into the world. Six months ago, she had thought this life she had chosen would be enough to satisfy the yearnings in the deepest part of her being, the part where she had buried dreams of family and her own forever love.

She'd been a fool.

She cherished each baby still, and knew herself blessed to be able to help these new mothers. But she also knew herself to be lonely. And all because Isaac had come into her life with his deep blue-gray eyes and his shy grin and had burrowed in her heart. Even six months later, her cheeks warmed at the thought of the way he had looked at her. And at the memory of the sweet kiss they had exchanged.

Stop it, Lizzy! She admonished herself for dwelling on things that could never be. Isaac was not Amish, and she would never leave her faith for a man. No matter how much she loved him. God must always come first.

Sometimes, though, staying the course hurt almost more than she could stand.

Cold, wet flakes hit her forehead and melted against the warmth of her cheeks. Casting her gaze to the late October sky, she blinked as more of the delicate flakes landed on her lashes, misting her vision. She was surprised to find that it had begun to snow while she was caught up in reminiscing. It hadn't been that cold when she had left the house that morning. She sniffed, appreciating the mingled scents of wood smoke and the cold air. Her heart was broken, but she could still find a small measure of cheer in the beauty around her.

After a few moments, she began to shiver as the cold sank deeper into her bones. She needed to stop woolgathering and get home. Her mother was making stew for dinner. Lizzy's stomach began to grumble with hunger as the thought of tasting her mother's cooking made her mouth water. Crossing her arms tight across her middle, she increased her pace; her boots made loud squishy noises as she trod on the road, still wet from the rain that had fallen the day before.

The wind kicked up, and her heavy black cloak flapped against her legs as she walked briskly toward the house where she still lived with her parents and younger siblings. She stomped through a puddle left from the day before, and winced, knowing her black stockings and the hem of her dark blue dress were now soaked. She could feel the wet stockings sticking to her legs.

Was it starting to snow where Isaac was? For a moment she allowed her thoughts to stray briefly to the man who had captured her heart so easily, despite all of her efforts to hold herself emotionally distant from him. She wondered if he was outside in the cold, or if he was sitting in his patrol car. Was he safe, or was he doing something in the line of duty that was putting his life in danger?

Was he feeling as lonely as she was? Even though they had both made their own choices, her heart ached that he might be suffering or unhappy.

Or maybe he was getting on with his life just fine without her. Startled by the thought that flashed across her mind, she halted, ignoring the wet mix of rain and snow that continued to pelt her. She didn't want him to be unhappy, but nor did she want him to forget her, to forget the brief time they had together.

Enough! She had to stop this. If she kept dwelling on him, she would only make herself miserable.

Lizzy knew the truth, though. She was already miserable. She did everything she was supposed to do. She followed the rules and she lived a good life; she went on house calls when it was necessary, she loved her family with her whole heart and she did her best to be a help to her mother.

Deep in her soul, though, she woke up every morning yearning to see the man who had made her pulse race. And she went to bed each and every night a little sadder that another day had passed without any word from him. Not that she expected one. She didn't. And even if she had once harbored the idea that she might see him again, she knew that it was impossible. She didn't even fool herself into believing that just seeing him one more time would be enough. She wanted him for life. It broke her heart, the knowledge that she would never be his wife.

Shaking herself out of her morose thoughts, she

quickened her pace once more as she rounded the bend, and her family's farmhouse rose into view, almost as if it just appeared out of nothing. She bent her head, allowing her black bonnet to take the brunt of the falling precipitation, and trudged up the gravel driveway to the front porch. With her head down, she had climbed three of the six steps before she realized someone was standing on the porch in front of her.

A masculine pair of legs covered in dark trousers stood before her. Briefly, she thought it was one of her older brothers, and she frowned, annoyed that he was standing in her way. She raised her face to tell her brother to move so she could get into the house before she froze to death. As her eyes traveled up to his face, however, all thoughts of complaining stuttered to a halt.

The thick blond hair fell just a hint too short to fit in with the Amish men she knew. Almost as if the wearer was growing it out from a very short hairstyle. The face below the wide-brimmed hat was clean-shaven, indicating that he was single. Barely daring to breathe, she forced herself to meet those blue-gray eyes that she had dreamed about for so many months, afraid to believe the truth of what her vision was telling her.

They gazed back at her, earnest, as if he could convince her of his purpose by his glance alone. The familiar warmth was there, without the wall that had always stood between them.

Isaac was back, and he was Amish.

Joy threatened to break free; she chained it down, fettering its wings inside her chest. She couldn't give in to it, not yet. Not until she knew that he was committed to staying. To the church and to her. She moved up the last three steps, then stopped.

"Liz."

The sound of her name in that husky voice broke some barrier in her heart. Tears gathered in her eyes and slipped out of the corners. They tracked down her cheeks. Isaac took a small step closer and wiped them away gently with his long fingers. A sob burst from her at the tenderness in his expression.

"Isaac," she gasped on a hiccup. "You're here. I didn't think I'd ever see you again. The way you're dressed— are you really Plain?"

"I am. Your *mamm* said we could talk undisturbed in the kitchen. Or we can stay here?" The last word came out in a question.

She was cold, and the kitchen would be more comfortable, but she didn't want to go inside yet. Even though *Mamm* said they could talk privately in the kitchen, she knew that the family was in the house. She wanted a few more minutes with him by herself before they took this visit indoors.

"We'll stay out here," he stated, clearly reading her intentions.

"You don't mind?"

He shrugged. "I don't care. As long as you and I iron some things out, I'm good standing in a full snowstorm."

She allowed a smile to tip the corners of her mouth as he took her hand and led her to the swing on the porch. It was still dry, so she sat down on it. Isaac didn't sit.

He leaned his back against the post on the porch and stretched his legs out in front of him.

"First, yes, I am Amish now. I quit my job four months ago and went home. I had several long talks with the bishop and we gave it a few months to make sure that joining the church was what I wanted. Don't be offended, Liz, but I knew that I couldn't join the church just so that I could marry you."

Her heart decided to climb up into her throat as she listened.

"You didn't join the church for me?" she asked, the opposite of offended. Living Plain took some sacrifice. He had to want the life, and not just her.

His glance swiftly scanned her expression. She smiled to encourage him to continue. He relaxed.

"*Nee.* I joined the church because God called me back home, and this is the life I want, whether you want me or not."

Her bruised heart was healing with every word. "I am so glad, Isaac. And I do. I do want you."

He flashed her the grin she remembered. "Good. Because I am in love with you, Elizabeth Miller. Would you marry me?"

Before she could blink, he was sitting on the swing beside her, offering her his hand, and his heart.

"Isaac, I love you, too. *Jah*, I will be your wife."

EPILOGUE

The sun wasn't even up yet when Lizzy slipped from her bed. She was far too excited to sleep any longer. She hadn't thought this day would ever arrive, but it was finally here. Dressing quickly, she hurried down the stairs to assist with the early-morning chores for her last time as a single woman. She headed out to the barn to milk the cows.

Today was the day that she would become Isaac's wife. She grinned.

Returning to the house, she saw that more women were in the kitchen with her mother. A quick breakfast was served, then she went upstairs to get ready for the service. Lizzy donned the purple dress she'd wear for her wedding. She had made it, of course. Her *mamm* had smiled at her through tears when she had seen it on Lizzy two days before.

"Ack! I am a foolish woman, *jah*? I thank *Gott* that you found a *gut* man like Isaac. Your *dat* and I have prayed for you to find someone."

Lizzy understood. Her fears and her anxiety had

caused her parents much concern, for they worried she'd end up alone and sad. Lizzy tugged on the apron she'd made and pulled on the black boots. A black bonnet went on over her everyday prayer *kapp*. She was ready.

She could hear the guests beginning to arrive. The service would start precisely at eight-thirty, and be held outside in the barn. Partly because there were going to be far more people coming than just the normal twenty families in their district. Isaac's family and many of the members of his community had traveled to attend the wedding.

And then there would be bleachers set up outside of the barn for their non-Amish guests. The bishop had granted permission for Isaac's former police colleagues to attend. She had no doubt that Ryder and Isaac would remain friends, even though Isaac was no longer a police officer. The bishop had also given Isaac permission to continue breeding and training dogs. Ryder, she knew, hoped to convince his chief to let him work with one of Isaac's dogs.

In addition to the cops, Rebecca and her husband, Miles, were in attendance with their son. Lizzy smiled thinking of her sister. Rebecca had confirmed to her privately that she and Miles would be having a second child in the spring. Amish women generally didn't share that news, but Rebecca and Lizzy had been through so much together that they had no secrets.

A mere three and a half hours later, Lizzy was standing beside her new husband. He looked dashing in his black suit and white shirt, accompanied by a new bow tie.

"What are you thinking, Lizzy, that has you smiling?" Isaac whispered, his warm breath tickling her ear.

"I am thinking that I am blessed. And—" she tossed him a flirtatious wink "—that when we are alone, I will have one last opportunity to feel your jaw without whiskers."

He blushed slightly, but winked back. He had shaved his beard for the last time this morning. From here on out, he would allow his beard to come in as a sign that he was a married man, although he would continue to shave off his mustache.

Rebecca and Miles approached them.

"Where's my nephew?" Lizzy signed and voiced at the same time for her husband's benefit.

"He's with his doting grandmother," Miles responded.

Raising a single eyebrow, Lizzy looked around for her mother. Martha Miller was indeed proudly showing off her grandson, Connor.

"Someday, she'll be doing that with our children," Isaac murmured, and it was her turn to blush.

"Beheef dich," she whispered fiercely, telling him to behave himself. He merely grinned back at her.

Soon, Martha called out, *"Cumme esse!"*

"Mamm says it's time to eat," Lizzy signed to her sister.

Isaac took her hand and led the way into the house to the seats of honor in the corner of the living room where tables had been set up. Not all the guests would eat at the same time. She and Isaac were in the first group. Although she wasn't exactly sure how much she would actually be able to eat today. Her stomach was still full of butterflies. She sat on Isaac's left. Just as she had watched *Mamm* sit on *Dat's* left in the buggy all the years of their married life. The women were seated on her side of the table, and the men were seated on Isaac's side.

"You know, in the *Englisch* world, couples sit together. There is no separation of the women and men," Isaac informed her.

"*Jah*, I know that." She shrugged. "I like our way."

He nodded. "Yeah, but I'm happy to sit next to you today. Have I told you how beautiful you are today?"

Happiness filled her. "I'm glad. I wanted you to be pleased."

"I'm more than pleased," he responded, his gaze warm. "I'm blessed beyond all my dreams. I have my faith back, have reconciled with my family and have been granted the gift of marrying a woman I love with my entire self."

"Oh, Isaac. I thought that this blessing would pass me by. But *Gott* knew that I needed a special man. He knew I needed you. I love you so much."

Later, when she had stepped outside after the evening meal, Isaac joined her in the shadows. He turned her toward him and bent, kissing her lightly. Her pulse pounded in her ears. She brought her hand up to trace his strong jaw. Tears spurted to her eyes as she felt the slight scratch of whisker stubble there. The joy bubbled up inside at the tactile sign that he was now her *mann*.

She leaned her head against his shoulder and closed her eyes on a sigh. God was so good. Soon, they would make their way to Ohio, where they would live with his mother. Lizzy knew that couples usually stayed near the bride's family, but she had told Isaac that she wanted to move. It was true. He had been apart from his family for so long, and his mother was a widow.

Moving to Ohio would also be a new start for her, a sign that her past was truly over.

They would come to LaMar Pond often enough to visit. And she knew that Rebecca and Miles would be frequent visitors.

She was content.

* * * * *

If you enjoyed this book, don't miss the other heart-stopping Amish adventures from Dana R. Lynn's Amish Country Justice series:

Plain Target
Plain Retribution
Amish Christmas Abduction
Amish Country Ambush
Amish Christmas Emergency

Find more great reads at www.LoveInspired.com.

Dear Reader,

If you're like me, you love visiting new places and meeting new people. There's something fascinating about it. That's how the Amish Country Justice series has felt to me. I have gotten to know and love the characters in LaMar Pond. Including Lizzy Miller, whom we met in Plain Retribution. *Guarding the Amish Midwife* was a little bittersweet for me. Although I loved seeing a few old characters, I also left LaMar Pond to journey to a new town.

Waylan Grove is a fictional town in Holmes County, Ohio. I look forward to exploring it with you. It is home to some interesting characters. Such as Isaac Yoder. Isaac and Lizzy both had some issues to work through before they found their happy ending. I enjoyed watching them find their way to each other.

I hope you enjoyed Lizzy and Isaac's story. As always, I love to hear from readers. You can find me at www.danarlynn.com. I am also on Facebook, Twitter and Instagram.

Blessings,
Dana R. Lynn

Get 4 FREE REWARDS!

We'll send you 2 FREE Books plus 2 FREE Mystery Gifts.

Love Inspired® Suspense books feature Christian characters facing challenges to their faith... and lives.

FREE Value Over $20

YES! Please send me 2 FREE Love Inspired® Suspense novels and my 2 FREE mystery gifts (gifts are worth about $10 retail). After receiving them, if I don't wish to receive any more books, I can return the shipping statement marked "cancel." If I don't cancel, I will receive 4 brand-new novels every month and be billed just $5.24 each for the regular-print edition or $5.74 each for the larger-print edition in the U.S., or $5.74 each for the regular-print edition or $6.24 each for the larger-print edition in Canada. That's a savings of at least 13% off the cover price. It's quite a bargain! Shipping and handling is just 50¢ per book in the U.S. and 75¢ per book in Canada.* I understand that accepting the 2 free books and gifts places me under no obligation to buy anything. I can always return a shipment and cancel at any time. The free books and gifts are mine to keep no matter what I decide.

Choose one:
- ☐ **Love Inspired® Suspense Regular-Print** (153/353 IDN GMY5)
- ☐ **Love Inspired® Suspense Larger-Print** (107/307 IDN GMY5)

Name (please print)

Address   Apt. #

City   State/Province   Zip/Postal Code

Mail to the Reader Service:
IN U.S.A.: P.O. Box 1341, Buffalo, NY 14240-8531
IN CANADA: P.O. Box 603, Fort Erie, Ontario L2A 5X3

Want to try 2 free books from another series! Call 1-800-873-8635 or visit www.ReaderService.com.

---

*Terms and prices subject to change without notice. Prices do not include sales taxes, which will be charged (if applicable) based on your state or country of residence. Canadian residents will be charged applicable taxes. Offer not valid in Quebec. This offer is limited to one order per household. Books received may not be as shown. Not valid for current subscribers to Love Inspired Suspense books. All orders subject to approval. Credit or debit balances in a customer's account(s) may be offset by any other outstanding balance owed by or to the customer. Please allow 4 to 6 weeks for delivery. Offer available while quantities last.

Your Privacy—The Reader Service is committed to protecting your privacy. Our Privacy Policy is available online at www.ReaderService.com or upon request from the Reader Service. We make a portion of our mailing list available to reputable third parties that offer products we believe may interest you. If you prefer that we not exchange your name with third parties, or if you wish to clarify or modify your communication preferences, please visit us at www.ReaderService.com/consumerschoice or write to us at Reader Service Preference Service, P.O. Box 9062, Buffalo, NY 14240-9062. Include your complete name and address.

LIS19R2

K-9 officer Gavin Sutherland held tight to his K-9 partner Tommy's leash and scanned the crowd, his mind on high alert, his whole body tense as he tried to protect the city he loved. People from all over the world stood shoulder to shoulder along the East River, waiting for the annual Fourth of July fireworks display.

His partner, a black-and-white springer spaniel, knew the drill. Tommy worked bomb detection. He had been trained to find incendiary devices. He knew to sniff the air and the ground. Sniff, sit, repeat. Be rewarded.

Glancing up, Gavin spotted his backup, K-9 officer Brianne Hayes, a rookie who had been paired with him to continue gaining experience.

Brianne headed toward him, her auburn hair caught up in a severe bun. That fire-colored hair matched her fierce determination to prove herself since she was one of only a few female K-9 officers in the city that never slept.

Brianne's partner, Stella, was also in training with the K-9 handlers.

"I've been along the perimeters of the park," Brianne said. "Nothing out of the ordinary. Can't wait for the show."

Scanning the area again, he said, "I think the crowd grows every year. Standing room only tonight."

"Stella keeps fidgeting and sniffing. She needs to get used to this."

Stella stopped and lifted her nose into the air, a soft growl emitting from her throat.

"Steady, girl. You'll need to contain that when the fireworks start."

But Stella didn't quit. The big dog tugged forward, her nose sniffing both air and ground.

Gavin watched the Labrador, wondering what kind of scent she'd picked up. Then Tommy alerted, going still except for his wagging tail that acted like a warning flag, his body trembling in place.

"Something's up," Gavin whispered to Brianne. "He's picked up a signature somewhere."

Brianne whispered low. "There's a bomb?"

Don't miss
Deep Undercover *by Lenora Worth,*
available July 2019 wherever
Love Inspired® Suspense books and ebooks are sold.

www.LoveInspired.com

Looking for inspiration in tales
of hope, faith and heartfelt romance?

Check out **Love Inspired®** and
Love Inspired® Suspense books!

New books available every month!